CYRUS
THE GREAT
AND HIS EMPIRE

His Triumph of Liberty and Freedom

F . G . G H A M S A R I

authorHOUSE

AuthorHouse™
1663 Liberty Drive
Bloomington, IN 47403
www.authorhouse.com
Phone: 833-262-8899

Published by AuthorHouse 01/22/2021

ISBN: 978-1-6655-1102-5 (sc)
ISBN: 978-1-6655-1101-8 (hc)
ISBN: 978-1-6655-1100-1 (e)

Library of Congress Control Number: 2020924926

DRA
Scripture taken from the Douay–Rheims Version of the Bible.

ESV
Unless otherwise indicated, all scripture quotations are from The Holy Bible,
English Standard Version® (ESV®). Copyright ©2001 by Crossway Bibles, a
division of Good News Publishers. Used by permission. All rights reserved.

Cyrus the Great and His Empire

Depictions in this book would propound a question, who had attacked our freedom that Cyrus had established for us? Was it Alexander the Great, Genghis Khan, Hitler or the appearance of many religions fighting among each other to proof their righteousness creating a world full of division and confusion?

The celebrated Persian poet Rumi lived 800 Years ago said, "I am not from here nor I am from there. I am not a Jew, a Christian, nor am I a Muslim…" Perhaps Rumi is detached from a nation, a religion or factors resulting in division, which is a poison to equality and freedom.

F. G. Ghamsari

To my wife, Monica; to my daughter, Jasmine Aryana, and all the members of my family-to all the people who sacrifice their lives to help others without monetary expectation or recognition-people who are working hard for freedom and economy-empowering the needy.

To Iran, which despite today's image brought freedom to humanity and it means the Aryan nation. Of course, today Aryan means the white people, which is completely different with its origin at the time of Cyrus the Great.

CONTENTS

PREFACE

I came across the story of Cyrus while publishing my first book in English, A Basket of Goodies. Issues discussed in the book related to justice, equality and predicaments facing many people in the world today. The more I read about Cyrus the more I wanted to learn, even though I had limited prior knowledge. It was especially interesting when the subjects in A Basket of Goodies were coherent with Cyrus's life story and gave me a reason to follow up.

I began searching websites for the most influential people in history. I searched extensively, but found only one site that mentioned Cyrus, and it had positioned him at the very end of the list. Most of the sites mentioned Alexander the Great, Genghis Khan, Hitler, whose destructions and killings of million innocent people would never be forgotten from history.

Yet, Cyrus who taught us the way to liberty and freedom was not acknowledging in majority of the websites. Beside those destructive leaders mentioned above, the websites had names with minor positive impact or some who negatively influenced the world. This lack or limited public knowledge about Cyrus the

Great, therefore, became the main reason for me to research and writing this book.

According to the sources I read, it was Cyrus, who was a military genius and conquered the world before any other rules. It was Cyrus, who virtually started our civilization centuries B.C. Moreover, it was Cyrus, who spoke of justice and equality before any other civil rights activists. How is it that his name is not mention among the most influential people in history?

Even though there are many books written about Cyrus and this book is not the first nor would be the last. The lack of public knowledge about Cyrus yet remains strong. This lack or limited public knowledge seems to be the reason for websites lacking Cyrus's name. It is, therefore, imperative to pass on our information about Cyrus the Great to others in order to pay our dues to the man, who originated for us the most valuable asset, liberty and human rights. However, in order to increase the public knowledge, perhaps we need more books, public speakers, articles, public education, and great movies made to introduce this marvelous leader, unique in history.

ACKNOWLEGMENT

An acknowledgment is due to the Greek historians particularly two of the most celebrated that without their effort to write history according to their visions, we would not have this amazing story to tell.

Among the great books written about Cyrus the Great, the most outstanding is *Cyropaedia* by Xenophon, a Greek physician and historian, who was fascinated by Cyrus, despite the rivalry. Alexander the Great and Julius Caesar both read this book, and Alexander studied it in his childhood; Cyrus was his idol. This book was also an inspiration for Thomas Jefferson.

Herodotus, who was called the "father of history", is another Greek historian who wrote extensively about Cyrus the Great and his triumphs in, *The History of Herodotus*.

An acknowledgment is due to my wife and my daughter, who paused their favorite TV episode to read my drafts expressing their opinions to impact my writings.

The public domain law is very clear and states that any work or image published before January 1923 is now in the public domain.

It means that any person can display the images without needing to obtain permission from anyone.

Nevertheless, many of the images that I intended to use were discarded because of copyright restrictions. Even though the images were published before 1923.

I am grateful to AuthorHouse, to facilitate for me to demonstrate limited images that were necessary as completive parts of the book. As the proverb is saying, "a picture is better than thousand words." How undoubtedly this statement is true.

Some of the images I had to discard are as follows, a portrait of Cyrus; Cyrus and his wife, Cassandane; moving crenate towers used by archers and war equipment; a scythed chariot; Cyrus among the Jewish prophets; Pasargadae architecture; Apadana Palace; a map of territories under the Persian Empire; and an image of the Cyrus Cylinder.

It is important to point out the time gap between the discarded images. For example, the image of Hebrew prophets by Jean Fouquet dates to 1470, or a marvelous image of Cyrus by Hamid Bahrami which was done in recent decades.

I am grateful and offer my congratulations to Reza Zarghamee for writing *Discovering Cyrus*; Farshad Abrishami for writing *Kourosh e kabir*; Behnam Muhammad Panah for writing *Zindegginameh e kourosh e Kabir*, as well as all other sources that helped me in writing this book about a man I truly admire and love.

I am also grateful to Leigh Allen and Rose Sheldon for coordinating systematically and assisting me whenever I needed assistance. I am thankful to Derrick Austin, whose encouragement and persistence guided me through.

I am thankful to Marna Poole for an excellent output of editing the manuscript word by word to coordinate it "largely on the style prescriptions of *The Chicago Manual of Style*", as Marna said. My humble gratefulness would also extend to the Editorial Service Team of AuthorHouse for their assistances.

Most of all I am greatly indebted to those who wrote about Cyrus and their writings were influential and the essential source to depend on establishing a story to tell. There were those predecessors from the ancient Greek historians to others throughout history compelling a profound story, which has been motivational and illuminating during history

INTRODUCTION

Ancient history covers a vast timeframe, from approximately the thirtieth century BC to around the fifth century AD. During these 3,500 years or more, one cannot imagine how many hundreds of leaders ruled over the nations or tribes. According to historians, however, only three leaders possessed qualities that were greater than all others during this vast period.

These three men, for better or worse, significantly changed the course of history. Therefore, here is a brief account of ancient history in a timely matter.

The tales of Zoroaster living in approximately 1000 BC; Noah and his ark; and tales of Abraham, Moses, David, Solomon, and so on are believed without much documentation, in many cases, giving us a view that these tales may or may not be true. In the hearts of believers, however, these stories are the words of God and are undoubtedly and undeniably the truth.

Nevertheless, the real ancient history in this book begins with Nebuchadnezzar, the tyrannical leader of Babylon, or around the Assyrian Empire. Therefore, we can begin with the Babylonians, the Egyptians, the Lydians, and the Medes, who shared the world among them. Intelligent humans lived on the earth from perhaps 60,000 BC or earlier, as evidence found in Iran indicates the existing of human life 100,000 BC, but because of the historians' lack of clarity, this period does not draw much concern.

The name of Nebuchadnezzar (630–561 BC)—creator of the Hanging Gardens of Babylon, one of the seven wonders of the ancient world, and the Tower of Babel—should be remembered. Due to his massacre of the Jewish tribe, he is frequently referred to in the Bible as an unfavorable person. Many Jewish prophets, however, believed his tyrannous behavior was the will of God and was a deserving punishment for those who did not follow the laws in the Hebrew book. History has not undermined Nebuchadnezzar's achievements.

The Lydian ruler Croesus and the Median king Astyages each had a long reign, although, historically, they were not among the important leaders. Meanwhile, the appearance of Cyrus the Great changed the course of history and gave a chance for an unknown tribe, the Persians, to dominate the world's politics, thus creating the first global empire.

Cyrus acquired most of the territories and established the Persian Empire, but his son Cambyses conquered Egypt and added it into the Persian Empire after Cyrus.

There is very little public knowledge about the Persians being the first most-developed civilization in the ancient history. Their sophistication in math and engineering resulted in their constructing some of the most amazing buildings in the world, lasting until today. Their ability to rule over vast territories—from Egypt to China and from the Indian Ocean to today's southern

Russia for over two centuries (559–330 BC) is a phenomenon that no other nation in history has ever achieved.

Cambyses, however, stayed too long in Egypt, and for some unknown reason, he either died or was killed. Thereafter, the royal court assigned Darius the Great to be the king. His kingdom's borders included Media, Babylon, Assyria, Elam, Greece, Egypt, Lydia, Armenia, Balkh, India, and Herat. His ambition was to facilitate roads and shorten sea travel, encouraging him to construct a canal between the Nile River and the Red Sea that enabled two ships to pass through at the same time—a historical landmark that eventually brought the Swiss Canal to the modern world. He reigned for thirty-five years (522–486 BC).

Xerox was another Persian king; he reigned for twenty-one years (486–465 BC). He conquered Athens in a war against the rebelling Greeks. After his victory, Xerox returned to Iran and oversaw the completion of the constructions in cities that his father had begun. Xerox married Esther and gave her the title of the Hebrew Queen Esther. Xerox learned of a political scandal and the reason behind it, and the vicious plot was subdued. Xerox ordered that the perpetrator be put to death. This action resulted in better and safer conditions for the Jews living in Iran.

After Xerox, the Persian Empire was the sole ruler of the world for approximately 130 years, until the appearance of Alexander the Great.

Perhaps this is good time to reveal the identity of the three greatest leaders throughout three and half millennia—Cyrus the Great (600–530 BC), Alexander the Great (356–323 BC), and Julius Caesar (100–44 BC). These leaders had one quality in common—their extraordinary military abilities. In looking at their accomplishments, we can see that each used his genius power to achieve his goals.

Although they were similar, each had a different character and unique personality. For example, Cyrus said, "Before me, my country was an unknown state in Asia. Now that I am dying, it is the largest country in the world." Alexander was extremely underpowered, but he found a way to defeat the mighty Persian military. Julius Caesar rose to power by his military ability and constant pursuit of his enemy. Cyrus created the freedom, Caesar created the calendar, and Alexander—I do not know what he created, besides distraction.

When Cyrus was fifteen years old, his father had to travel and crowned his son Cyrus, just in case he didn't return. Cyrus promised to support his father's kingdom and never announced his independence as long as his father was alive.

When Alexander was sixteen years old, his father, Philip, had to attend an affair abroad, and he left his son in charge. Alexander wanted to challenge his father's authority and superiority, and he wished to outdo his father.

Unlike his predecessors, whenever Cyrus conquered a foreign land, he commanded his soldiers to protect the safety of its citizens. He would tell them, "Do not harm the citizens or steal their belongings." His character when defeating civilians was so kind that he was immediately loved and welcomed in the countries that he conquered. When Cyrus was victorious over other rulers, he became friends with them and often brought them to live in Iran near him. His philosophy was not to collect wealth for himself but to let his friends have it. He said that his friends were his treasure, even until the last day of his life.

After victory in Babylon, Cyrus ordered that all gold, silver, and jewels, in the form of plates or cups or otherwise, that Nebuchadnezzar had brought to Babylon be taken back to Jerusalem. He encouraged the Jews to begin to build their temple in Jerusalem. Cyrus was highly ethical and kind, and he proclaimed the declaration of human rights and freedom of speech.

After victory in Persia, Alexander burned the largest library of the time, looted gold, silver, and jewels, then destroyed the capital city, Persepolis. He rushed to Pasargadae, to the burial site of Cyrus the Great, who had ruled the world centuries before him. Historians have said that Alexander took the mummified body of Cyrus out of his coffin disrespectfully, stole the historical jewels that Cyrus or his children had placed at his tomb, and left the body halfway hanging out of the coffin.

This story has a different version that Alexander visited the tomb of Cyrus to pay his respect to his role model. Because Alexander was on his way to India, he appointed guards to secure the tomb. When he returned from India, he saw that the guards had disrespected the body of Cyrus and stole the jewels. He severely punished them.

Whichever story is real does not change the fact that a mischief to one of the greatest historical monument accorded when Alexander visited the tomb of Cyrus. The beautiful gardens and historical sites in Pasargadae became an isolated desert. Moreover, after Alexander's visit, and later, the appearance of Islam, the body of Cyrus the Great as well as the memorial items entirely disappeared.

Many historians agree that Alexander had multiple personalities and could not be contain. He had some of his closest friends murdered as well.

Julius Caesar replaced the pharaoh in Egypt with Cleopatra, who became the queen of Egypt. History is fixated on this possibly romantic story and affair. Caesar killed many people in wars, especially in Germany. He also betrayed some of his closest friends. Although he was significantly important for advancements in the Roman Empire, he was a dictator. He also was busy with civil wars on one hand and with the powerful General Pompey on the other hand. Caesar was constantly behind the military forces and civil wars where there was not an absolute power. Therefore, his dictatorship led to his assassination by liberators when he was fifty-five. Caesar was one of the most important figures in the Roman Empire.

Who was the best leader among these three outstanding rulers? The choice is easy. We can either believe in the Word of God, revealed in the Bible, that Cyrus the Great was a king, guided by God, to carry out God's divine mission, or we can choose not to accept such a word.

Cyrus was an extraordinarily unique king who tried to stop the systematic tyrannical technique of pulling the eyes out of defeated nations and tribes by savage rulers throughout history. Cyrus the Great tried to show us and other leaders how to be a human being and how to be kind and considerate in our lives. The choice of who was the best leader is easy—the man who gave us freedom of speech, human dignity, and so much more.

It has been an absolute pleasure and honor for me to gather information concerning the life story of an extraordinary man, Cyrus the Great, king of the four corners of the world, king of kings, the Messiah, or the kindest king.

AUTHOR'S NOTE

When I saw the 2004 film Alexander, based on the life of Alexander the Great, I pondered that, for many reasons, Alexander was never great as was Cyrus. Therefore, I decided to write this book, a book that will reveal the life of a man so great and so kind that, even today, our lives benefit from what he did 2,500 years ago. Here it is—exactly what I wanted to say about that kind king, without ambiguity or doubt.

The most important event in Cyrus's life that interested me was his vision for the future and signing the first *declaration of human rights* in history. He was a ruler who emphasized in his speeches and actions the necessity to provide freedom and equal rights for all.

Cyrus the Great is an inspiring and unique historical figure that we can call him the most influential leader in history. Many reasons contribute to his uniqueness, unlike any other leader,

- He was saved by a shepherd against an order from the Median king to kill him at birth. The shepherd and his wife kept Cyrus's identity a secret.

- When Cyrus was ten years old, his identity accidentally was discovered. The Median king spared Cyrus's life and sent him to live with his parents in Persia.

- After his father's death, Cyrus became the king of the Persians and built the largest nation humankind had ever seen, where people with different ethnicities, races, colors, and religions lived freely in harmony and peace.

CHAPTER 1

Dreams of the Median King Astyages

It was the beginning of spring. The flowers were blooming and the cherry trees were covered with new leaves and blossoms. The songs of the birds, especially the nightingales, could be heard from far away. The fresh air blew from the mountains and the seas, preparing the Medes to celebrate their New Year festival, coming on the first day of spring

The mighty Median king Astyages was having this annual spring festival at his palace. He invited the royal and noble Medes to attend the ceremony and his celebration. His only daughter, Mandana, was responsible for assembling the musicians and the dancers and to see that, the event would go on in the best way possible.

It was not much after sunset when guests, one by one, accompanied by their family, entered the palace. At the entrance in the front yard was a large and wide gate, left open, inviting the guests to come in. Security guards guided the guests to walk along either side of the pool to enter the building.

Amazing flowers covered the wall inside, and apples, grapes, pears, and oranges decorated the corner tables. Wine was offered to the guests and especially to the king and his close friends. Guests were seated according to their ranks, with those of higher rank sitting closer to the king. Dinner was served, and dancers and musicians entertained the guests.

A little after midnight, the guests thanked the king respectfully, said good night, and left.

After the guests were gone, it was time for Astyages to go to bed. He'd had lots of fun but unintentionally had drunk wine and other alcohol barrages excessively.

He had a comfortable sleep, but just before sunrise, he had a frightening dream that woke him.

According to Herodotus the Greek historian, he summoned the magi, whose jobs were to interpret the king's dreams or to act as consultants when he needed advice. He told the magi that his dream was about his unmarried daughter, Mandana.

"From her stomach, an enormous amount of water flowed that submerged Ecbatana without difficulty."

One of the magi responded, "The greatness of your future grandson will be much greater than your own, which might occur at your expense."

In order to stop this prophecy, the frightened king decided to send his daughter away to Persia to marry Cambyses, who was harmless and without much military power. Astyages did not worry about Cambyses, whose kingdom was under his reign and who had asked Mandana to be his wife.

Consequently, several carriages, equestrians, and especial guards were prepared to accompany Mandana to Persia.

When the news traveled to Persia, a great ceremony was planned to welcome Mandana in Pasargadae. At her arrival, a joyfully marriage ceremony began. As was the custom, it lasted seven days and seven nights.

This solution seemed to be calmative for a while, and the predicament was subdued, until Astyages heard that his daughter was pregnant. Thinking so much about Mandana's pregnancy caused Astyages to have a second dream, which was more devastating to him than the first dream. He saw a vine sprout from Mandana, and it was so huge that it overshadowed all corners of the world. Immediately, he summoned the magi and described his dream in its entirety.

They said that his second dream was a continuation of the first dream, and one day, his unborn grandson would conquer his kingdom and would become the greatest king ever.

Fearful King Astyages sent a caravan and asked his pregnant daughter to visit Ecbatana. Mandana, who was homesick and without knowing her father's intentions, accepted the invitation, and a voyage was prepared to take her back to Ecbatana.

That is how the story begins.

The Birth of Cyrus

The eagles were flying high, the lions were roaring, the horses neighing, the monkeys jubilant, and the birds singing their songs, preparing the world for the upcoming birth of a child who would grow up to change the world like never before.

He would be titled the king of kings; the king who would be referred to by the Jewish Bible as the Messiah (Isaiah 45,1); king of Anshan; king of Babylon; king of Media; king of Persia; and the king of the four corners of the world; "the sun."

He would introduce freedom of speech and the first declaration of human rights. He would provide the first postal system, the circulation of currency, the first worldwide government, and the foundation of civilization and its advancement. He would construct interstate roads and so much more. Historians would refer to him as the most important leader ever.

Cyrus the Great was the first son of Cambyses, a lower-ranking king in Persia, and the first grandson of Astyages, a much higher-ranking king in Media. His mother, Mandana, was the only daughter of King Astyages of Media. She became an important part of a chessboard game of a dream that sent her to Persia to marry Cambyses, an insignificant political figure.

A Shepherd Miraculously Keeps Cyrus Alive

Shortly after Mandana returned to Ecbatana, her father placed her under house arrest, where she remained until she delivered her baby boy, whom she named Cyrus. Soon thereafter, Astyages spoke with his trusted friend Harpagus, telling him to take the infant far away and kill him.

Harpagus was like a son to Astyages. He had found his way into the court at very young age and had worked his way up to a point that no work was done without his permission or his direct involvement. Hence, this father-son relationship created a strong mutual trust. This was the reason that Astyages trusted Harpagus to accomplish this mission.

Harpagus, however, was aware that Astyages did not have any other children. He thought that when Astyages died, his daughter would become the queen, and if she found out that Harpagus had killed her first baby, she could punish him severely or even kill him. Cautiously, Harpagus took the infant and gave him to Mehrdad, one of the king's shepherds.

Harpagus told Mehrdad, "Leave this baby in the wilderness to die. After he is dead, bring me proof to show the king."

The shepherd also was reluctant to kill the child. He thought about the consequences and debated with himself over what to do. He fought with his conscience, and his conscience would not allow him to carry out the mission. It seemed that the entire world was angry, and it was blowing the hardest wind in his direction.

As Mehrdad held the baby in his arms, he developed a profound feeling for the baby. He thought about what to do and how he might escape from this sinful order. He leaned more definitively toward keeping the child, and so he decided to take him home. As he was lost in his thoughts on the future of the child, he finally arrived home.

He placed his animals in the barn and went to see his pregnant wife. He found her lying down because she was ill. He showed her the baby and told her of the king's desire and his own mission. He'd been unsure of how she would react to this news, but she was happy to see the baby. She informed her husband that she had given birth to a dead son. It was at that second that they looked at each other and decided they would keep the infant and raise him as their own son.

The next day, Mehrdad wrapped the stillborn baby in the prince's clothes and took the dead child to Harpagus as proof.

Harpagus, who did not want to spend much time on the matter, then reported to the king that his throne was safe.

One might wonder about such a vicious wish by King Astyages and his strange desire. How could a grandfather have a death wish for a grandson because the child might one day obtain greatness that surpassed the king's own greatness? There are two possible reasons for such unorthodox behavior, (1) King Astyages was an ill-minded person and a selfish individual who did not want his greatness besmirched; or (2) King Astyages was a proud king who wanted the superiority of the Medes to continue over other tribes; he wanted nothing to disturb their domination over the Persians and other tribes.

Mehrdad and his wife, however, gave a new name to the prince and kept his identity a secret.

There in the mountains, Cyrus mastered horseback riding when he was five or six years old, often without a saddle. While he was growing up in the mountains, nobody knew who he really was. In fact, he himself did not know that he was the beneficiary of two kingdoms. He had a very simple life with the shepherd and his wife, occasionally hunting and helping with the livestock. At the playgrounds, children of noble families called him the shepherd's son, and that is who he was—until he was ten years of age.

The Turning Point in Cyrus's Life

When Cyrus was ten years old, he became a playmate with the children of the royal family. During play, because of his attractive physical appearance, the children elected him as their king. All of them accepted his authority and obeyed his commands, but one boy refused to accept him as king whenever they played. Cyrus, as the "king," had no choice but to punish the boy. The obstinate, selfish boy cried to his father, who was a close friend of the king.

Angrily, boy's father took the matter to his friend, King Astyages and asked, "How is it that a shepherd's son can punish my son, a member of the royal family?"

Without a delay, the king commanded that the boy be brought forth, as well as his father. When they arrived, the king asked, "How did you have the courage to have such outrage behavior with my friend's son?"

"I did nothing wrong, sir," Cyrus replied. "We were playing a game in the village, and he was among us. Because they thought that I was the most qualified, they made me their king, but he did not obey me. If I did something wrong, I am ready for the consequences."

As Cyrus spoke, Astyages noted the resemblance between his own features and the boy's. He became suspicious and thought that the boy might be his grandson. He asked Mehrdad, "Whose boy is this? How did he come in your possession?"

The shepherd said, "This boy is mine and his mother's."

Astyages put the shepherd under the torture and told him, "If you do not speak the truth, I will sentence you to death."

Mehrdad was tortured so much that he finally confessed and explained how the prince came to him. Mehrdad begged the king for his life.

The king forgave him and said, "Because of your honesty and your true confession, you can go home a free man and do not have to worry about anything."

Astyages was extremely angry, but he did not show his anger. He summoned the magi and requested their opinion.

One of them said, "There will not be any harm to you because Cyrus has showed his greatness at playground, which satisfies the prophecy."

Harpagus soon learned of the day's events and became frightened. Without hesitation, he appeared before the king, saying, "Your Majesty, on one hand, I wanted to obey your order to have the infant killed, but on the other hand, I did not want to be responsible for killing your grandson and your daughter's first child. I gave the boy to Mehrdad and told him to leave the baby in the wilderness to die." Then, Harpagus asked for forgiveness.

The king, concealing his anger, granted Harpagus's wish.

Harpagus fell on the ground and thanked the king for sparing his life.

Harpagus had no idea of Astyages's vicious plan when the king said, "I also am grateful. I was angry at myself for directing you to kill my daughter's son, my only grandson. We have to thank the Lord that Cyrus is here among us. I also am glad that I do not have the tragedy of ending my line with my daughter."

The king then ordered for gathering, saying, "We have to

prepare for a celebration today." He asked Harpagus to send his thirteen-year-old son to play with Cyrus.

When the Harpagus's son arrived, the king slew him and prepared a meal, using his meat. When Harpagus arrived, the king served him the boy's meat and asked, "How is your meal, Harpagus? Is the meat delicious?"

Harpagus replied, "It was very good."

Then the king's servants brought out a covered basket for Harpagus. The king asked Harpagus to uncover the basket.

Harpagus almost passed out when he saw the head and hands of his son in the basket. This unbearable tragedy seeded a great hatred in Harpagus's heart for the king, but he concealing his hatred and said, "Whatever the king wishes is good."

Astyages Sends Cyrus to Live with His Parents in Persia

A convoy was prepared to send Cyrus to his parents in Persia. Astyages showered him with gold and fine presents and told him that he was welcome anytime that he desired to come back.

When Cyrus arrived in Persia, the biggest celebration and chanting began for the prince, lasting for days. He told his parents all about his past and all about the adventures in his life. He was thankful to the shepherd and his wife for taking care of him for so many years, and he was thankful that they had saved his life. He was also thankful to the shepherd for teaching him all skills that he knew while he was living with Mehrdad and his wife as their son. In addition, he was grateful that Mehrdad had taught him to be such a good hunter and an excellent horseman. Most of all, he was grateful that finally he had found his real mother and father, his roots, and his real family. Before long, Cyrus became the most popular, bravest young man throughout the country.

Then, it was time for the prince to pursue his education.

According to Xenophon the Greek physician and the historian, Cyrus's education in Persia included schooling offered to the sons of nobles, as well as early learning of the hardships of wars. In his father's court, he learned customs and manners, including high ethics, human dignity, and fairness. He learned difficult fighting techniques and many human behavioral traits that were different in Persia than in other places. The young prince was always eager to learn something new. When he engaged in competition, he was fair and respectful. He had an amazing ability to ride horses, and he was extremely respectful to his elders.

At center of the city where Cyrus was living and growing up, there was a square, where governmental offices such as the courts and the administrative offices were located. The square was divided into different sections, and one section belonged to children's education and training. The children's program was intended to prepare them to defend the city, which was their national honor.

In order to participate in the educational program, children were required to follow several behavioral requirements, such as not lying, avoiding rebellious acts, being fair and just, avoiding jealousy, avoiding bullying, and retaining good behavior.

Xenophon said that the Persians taught their children the value of life, to appreciate what they had, and to be grateful for whatever that they received. Highway robbery, resisting the law, theft, and profanity were considered sins that would be followed with punishments.

Children between the ages of ten and sixteen had a duty to stay in the city and to learn how to protect the center of the city and the government offices. Every month, half of them had a chance to go hunting with the king. The other half would stay to protect the city, following their education. Those elected to go hunting had to bring an arrow, a shield, and a sword. The importance of the hunting program was to teach children how to deal with hot and cold weather and with thirst and hunger and how to attack, crawl, and run. This program made children strong and taught them how to escape danger.

When they reached the age of sixteen or seventeen, they no longer were considered children; then, they entered different programs among the other youths. Young men who had completed ten years of training as well as the required duties would enter different programs with men until they were twenty-five years old. At this age, they would obtain important jobs in different fields, including protecting the country or administrative jobs. Men who reached fifty years of age were retired from the force but remained in city to teach all that they had learned during their lifetimes to the youths.

Cyrus's Training and Education in Persia

While in Persia, Cyrus learned lying and stealing were forbidden and sinful. There, the young prince learned at an early age to be kind, trustful, generous, polite, and fair to all. These qualities earned Cyrus love and respect among the public and the heads of the Persian tribe.

In order to be a great king, Cyrus had to gain proper skills in human dignity and religious concepts. He also needed to become a great warrior.

Cyrus possessed a unique talent for education; particularly, he had a hankering to acquire knowledge in law.

Historians said, one day, he came home and told his mother that he was glad that he had been reprimanded by his teacher when he could not resolve a dispute.

"A tall boy was wearing a coat that was too small," Cyrus, told her. "He exchanged it, forcefully, for the larger coat of a shorter boy. I recommended that each boy keep the coat that fit him best. My instructor disagreed because his duty is to convey the justice instead of the fashion. The shorter boy had the right to his own coat, as he had bought it for himself. My instructor taught me that what is lawful is just, and an act of violence is always unlawful. So, Mother, you see I have justice in my hands."

Sometimes, it was painful for Cyrus to see that his father did not have the power or the greatness of his grandfather Astyages. One day, Cyrus was riding with his usual guard, who told him that his father was a small king.

Cyrus moved his fist into the air and said, "I am the son of a great king. Why did you say a small king?"

The guard replied, "I have seen the Median king who has a great country, with people who speak different languages. I concluded that he must be a great king. But your father is king to a country that is much smaller, where everybody speaks the same language."

The young prince was amazed by the guard's knowledge. Later that day, he asked his father for the truth.

Cambyses thought a while and then said, "I am Cambyses, and this land that I have—with great horses and good people—the Lord has granted me. With his assistance, I will protect it."

Cyrus listened and was convinced at that time, but years later, he was not happy with his father's answer. Cyrus had learned that the most important quality of a man is his honesty and truthfulness.

As Xenophon said, Cyrus and other boys sat on wooden benches, listening to the poets who told stories about their ancestors' land, Iran. The poets ensured that they had the boys' attention so that Cyrus would not forget that he was an Aryan, a rider, and a conqueror. Cyrus listened to the verses that spoke of the sun, as well as listening to the philosophy of numbers. He was forced to solve mathematical problems and answer complicated questions.

The time came for Cyrus to go to Ecbatana, Media, to visit his grandfather, the mighty Median king, after many years. Cyrus generally didn't go to Media; it was his customary practice to spend his time in Persia. After his first visit, however, it became normal that he was sent to Media to spend time with Astyages as well.

Visiting His Birthplace, Ecbatana

Cambyses and Mandana prepared a voyage for their son to visit his grandfather. Guards on horseback, carriages, and workers accompanied the prince to Media. It was two days and one night, after frequent sightseeing, before they arrived.

Astyages was in his palace, waiting for Cyrus. He was very happy to see his grandson and took him around to show him different parts of his palace. Each room was decorated better than the other, with amazing silk curtains and colorful rugs. Outside, at the center of the front yard, was a large swimming pool, decorated with exotic flowers all around it. Plants and fancy trees covered other parts of the yard, and a few colorful peacocks gracefully walked on both side of the pool. In the backyard were apple, fig, and other fruit trees, each so covered with fruit that the branches were bent to the ground. The most amazing horses were kept in the stable, and chickens, cows, and other animals were in the barn.

Cyrus was brave, and he loved adventure. Although he was not even fifteen years old, he asked his grandfather, "Could I go hunting in the wild instead of hunting in an enclosed park here?"

Astyages allowed his request but said, "Obey the instructions of the guards, and be careful."

The young prince agreed, but once he was in the field, he forgot all about his promises. He began chasing a deer while riding his horse down a slope. He almost stumbled off the horse, but he managed to shoot his arrow killing the deer. He dismounted from his horse to see his deer. When the guards arrived, even though they were amazed by the prince's bravery, they told Cyrus that he had put himself in a great danger.

Cyrus asked them to allow him to confess and report the incident to the king. The king was pleased when heard about the incident.

Cyrus was very happy to have had a chance to visit his grandfather, as well as Ecbatana, where he had spent his childhood, but it was time for him to go back to Persia. Astyages showered his grandson with jewels, numerous horses, and many fine gifts.

Rather than keeping the gifts, Cyrus began giving them away to his friends and to those who gathered along his way to wish him farewell.

Discouraged, Astyages told him, "The gifts were for you only and for your enjoyment."

The popular prince responded, "Allow me to keep my head high the next time that I come back to you."

Then he asked the king for his permission to allow his friends to keep the gifts. Astyages agreed to his request. Cyrus gave away even his own coat that he was wearing.

At that early age, Cyrus understood that his role was not only to command but also to provide for those beneath him. He also knew that he needed to be affirming and to use his authority to bring subordinates in line.

Cyrus's Ancestors and His Marriage to Cassandane

When Cyrus was a young man, he came in contact with an extraordinarily beautiful young woman named Cassandane. He like her even more when he noticed that she often sent food or fruits to Mehrdad, the shepherd, who took care of him when he was a child.

Cassandane was from a royal Persian family, and her father owned a large cherry orchard on the other side of the river. Cyrus, with his short reddish-blond hair, just like a lion, often went watch her as she picked cherries. Cassandane, far away across the river, would offer him some cherries, but her voice was lost in the river's waves. Sometimes, she joked around with him as well.

One day, Cyrus went to see her and gave her his sword buckle as a gift. She shined it every day, whenever that she had a chance.

Eventually, at a large royal ceremony, Cyrus raised Cassandane's hand and announced that she was going to be his wife, despite his father's having had a different dream and wanting Cyrus to have a wife from Media to expand his power. When he saw so much joy in his son's face, however, he was happy and accepted the marriage.

This was the biggest event for the Persians for as long as they could remember. Many people came to celebrate this union from different places. The festival was open to the public from every level of the society.

Their marriage was so powerful that Cassandane accompanied Cyrus in all battles. Cassandane and Cyrus had four children— two daughters and two sons. Sadly, she died in Babylon from an illness that she contracted on the battlefield.

Cyrus was descended from two lines of the kingdom. From his mother, he was Median, and from his father, he was Persian. He inherited his throne from his father, a Persian king. Therefore, he considered himself a Persian king as well as a Median and from many tribes. He did not favor one Aryan tribe over another and made them all united to become the largest empire ever. He also divided the jobs equally and fairly between the tribes. The administrative jobs mostly were given to the Medes because they had prior experience.

After Cyrus united the Aryan tribes, he organized the kingdom committee, with seven noble members from different tribes. As he had the majority vote, he became the chairperson.

The king and the Kingdom Committee or the War Council

CHAPTER 2

Inheriting the Persian Throne

Cyrus inherited the Persian throne in Pasargadae after his father passed away. He already had succeeded to the throne years before, but out of respect to his father, he did not practice his independence until his father's death.

Cyrus was fifteen years old when his father had to deliver horses and gifts to Astyages. Before his departure, he called the heads of the tribe and his administrators to announce that Cyrus was his successor.

To respect his father, Cyrus put his head down, placed his hand in his father's hand, and said, "I will serve and protect my father wholeheartedly and never do anything to harm his kingdom."

It was customary for Persian kings to announce their successors when they went away to war or they had to take a long trip. Thus, Cambyses did exactly what he needed to do. In this transition of power, Cyrus's behavior spoke of trust and an extraordinary honesty in the young prince.

Cyrus was healthy, smart, well built, and good-looking. He

was plain and humble, with great communication skills and social-connection ability. His education in Persia and at his grandfather's court enabled him to be likable and extremely stable.

Wine drinking in the royal court was the norm, although Cyrus did not care for it and did not agree with drinking wine, especially in excess. He believed that wine would disable the mind.

The Just Warrior, Cyrus, Becomes the King of Persia

Cyrus became the king when his father died in 551 BC. In the beginning, he had no desire to raise the Persians against the Medes, though he never liked his father's political position of accepting the Median domination.

As historians stated, Harpagus never forgot his son's tragic beheading. When Cyrus became the king, Harpagus found an opportunity to take his revenge on Astyages. He began to communicate with Cyrus and often sent him gifts. Harpagus knew Cyrus's strength and abilities. As he witnessed the overwhelming dissatisfaction among the heads of the Medes toward Astyages, Harpagus wrote a letter to Cyrus and reminded him of the time that Astyages had planned to kill him,

"God will protect you, and you will become the greatest king of our nations. Remember that Astyages wanted to kill you. If today you are alive, it is first because of the will of God and second that I did not carry out your grandfather's command and, instead, entrusted you to the shepherd. If you trust me, you will become the greatest king ever. Raise the Persians against the Medes. Most likely, I will be the war commander, and then I will help you to victory. Everything is ready for you."

When Cyrus became aware of contents of the letter, he considered Harpagus's recommendations and decided to do just what he suggested. He ordered that the brush and bushes be cleared off from a large field, and he invited the heads of the tribes and the public to gather for an announcement.

He ordered that his father's cows be killed and prepared food for the people who were expected to gather. A large crowd accepted his invitation and showed up, but he saw an assemblage of people, such that never had gathered before in Persia.

After serving the food and wine, Cyrus asked in a loud voice, "Are you prepared to be free and to be happy, or do you want to always work hard without any happiness?"

He convinced the public that they must end the domination by the Medes because that would result in their freedom and happiness. Cyrus's speech was so effective that the Persians, who hated the Median domination, validated the points their leader had made and accepted his invitation to face the Medes.

Defeating the Medes; Uniting the Aryan Tribes

Information about this gathering soon traveled to Media and was revealed to Astyages, who organized a huge, well-trained army, consisting of archers and cavalries. The most fearful were the Scythians, who settled northwest of Iran. Saka hordes were another force on horseback, capable of swarming columns of infantry in an open field.

Meanwhile, Astyages wanted to stop the Persian rebellion before it could become strong and dangerous. He asked Harpagus to be the lead commander in the forthcoming battle. On the Persian side, Cyrus himself was to lead the army, which was much smaller in number than the Median army.

Finally, it came the time for the forces to meet, and when they did, many Median soldiers—deliberately and without a fight—joined Cyrus's military. The other Median soldiers, who now were outnumbered, found themselves in the dangerous condition of facing death or serfdom, and they ran away. King Astyages was furious when he heard the news. He first gathered the magi, who had interpreted his dreams incorrectly. He beheaded them, and then he prepared a new army for his second attack.

It was difficult for him, at his older age, to personally participate in the fighting; hence, he was defeated easily and captured.

When Harpagus saw that the king had been captured, he could not resist his joyful feelings. He went up to the king and said, "Remember the day that you slew my son and served me his meat? It is difficult for me to recall and it's painful. I carried the pain all my life, but now that you are a hopeless, captive prisoner, you must feel much worse than I ever did."

Astyages looked at him and replied, "You are a worthless fool who has no conscience. I know that you caused our defeat. You had the highest position in Media, but you could not see our greatness over the other tribe. Now we will be a satellite, following the Persians. You have no pride."

Cyrus did not impose hardship to Astyages. He enforced the most respectful treatment for the king.

After thirty-five years, the kingdom of Astyages ended, and so did 128 years of Median domination over the Aryan tribes in Iran.

CHAPTER 3

Attacking Croesus, the Lydian King

Lydia was a country located west of Asia Minor or where Turkey is located today, plus territories that are more western. Lydia was super-rich because of its gold and silver mines, natural resources, and its important sea/land position internationally.

According to Herodotus, King Croesus had just accepted the throne, and he was following in his father's footsteps, expanding Lydia's territories. He seized all Greek-occupied territories located in Asia Minor, except for Miletus, which kept its independence by paying an annual fee to the Lydians. Hence, the sea connection remained in the hands of the Greeks, as long as they paid their taxes to Lydia. Therefore, Lydia became a center of trade, in particular in its capital city of Sardis.

The relationship between the Greeks and the Lydians blossomed, and this mutual friendly atmosphere facilitated travel between them. Sardis became a center of science, philosophy, business, and wealth. It drew many scientists and the Athenian philosopher, political mastermind, and diplomat Solon, who became a close friend with Croesus.

One day, Croesus asked Solon, "Who is the most prosperous person in the world?" Croesus expected Solon to answer that it was Croesus.

Solon, however, responded, "It depends on the last days of one's life."

The environment created such wealth for Croesus that his name became a mythical proverb across Greece and Asia Minor. He was so rich that the Greeks referred to his wealth as the treasure of Croesus.

Sardis's treasury was the largest gold repository in the ancient world. The gold was not just ingots and coins but also in the form of art. This abundant wealth made Croesus think of expanding his territories even farther. He thought it was necessary to hire soldiers from Greece. To facilitate his idea, he built a golden lion statue at the Delphi temple that weighed 573 pounds. He built an Apollo statue to satisfy a friendly relationship with the Spartans, with an agreement to hire the needed soldiers from the Spartans as well.

Lydia always had retained a peaceful relationship with the Medes, but when Croesus heard of the fall of the Medes, he thought that it was the best time to pursue his dream.

The Greeks and the Spartans were in his corner. He sent a message to Amasis, the Egyptian pharaoh, and to the tyrannical king of Babylon, asking for assistance.

It was not very long before he received positive responses from both. He became convinced that with his abundant weapons and international help that he quickly would be victorious. He did not think much of Cyrus, who had united the Aryan tribes under one kingdom. He thought that the new king was either a puppet of the Medes or someone who was inexperienced in global affairs.

In order to begin the battle, he consulted with biggest temple—Apollo, Amman, Dodona, and others, requesting guidance on whether to pursue his idea. The answer he received was not what he wanted to hear, but it didn't matter; he had already made up his mind.

In addition to his own cavaliers, archers, generals, soldiers, and the help from the Greeks and the Spartans, Croesus had the Egyptian soldiers on their way as well. Hence, he was ready to move his men for an attack. The news traveled by a man named Eurybates and was revealed to Cyrus.

Cyrus sent a peaceful message to Croesus, requesting that he reevaluate his decision.

The response came back: "The Persians need to be the slaves, as they were the slaves of the Medes."

Despite Cyrus's reluctant sentiments and negative feelings, as he had just terminated a war with the Medes, another war for Cyrus was on the horizon. He would defend his honor as well as the land, which he dearly loved. The Lydians and the Greeks were superstitious. Cyrus and his generals put this knowledge to good use when they fought hard to establish Persian rule over Lydia.

Croesus and his full forces were on their way to Iran. Nevertheless, Cyrus decided that it was not to his advantage to travel hundreds of miles outside of Iran to face the enemy in a land that he did not know anything about. Thus, he waited.

Croesus had to cross the Halys River, which was overflowing

with excessive rainwater. Crossing the river, especially without a bridge, was difficult. They created different branches and diverted the water flow in various directions, which enabled them to cross.

Eventually, Croesus arrived at Pteria, a city on the shores of the Black Sea. Savagely, Croesus plundered and robbed the belongings of the city's population and made them his slaves.

It was not long before the well-prepared Cyrus arrived at the east side of Pteria as well. He divided his army into two sections and appointed Arasp to command one section and Vishtasb, Darius's father, to command the other.

Cyrus himself planned assertive programs and made assessments to secure the implementations of his plans. He ordered the lancers to be at the first line and the archers to be behind them. He also ordered the soldiers to loudly sing epic songs, and told them that at their backs would be a moving caravan, carrying weapons, so that any time they needed weapons, they could acquire them.

When Cyrus saw that his men were ready, he made a moving speech to them.

First, however, he sent a message to the Greek and Spartan soldiers: "You can leave the war zone before the fight begins, and I will forgive you."

They did not accept this offer and refused to leave. Cyrus again sent a peaceful message to Croesus, promising that his kingdom and his family in Sardis would be safe, and they could stay friends.

The ambitious, miscalculating Croesus had rated Cyrus ineffective and an instrument of the Medes, so he rejected the offer.

Croesus ordered a head-on attack toward the center, but

Cyrus's attack was from left first and then from the right side. When the battle began, Cyrus began singing an epic song, which his soldiers quickly repeated.

The Persian forces included ten thousand fighting cavaliers, one hundred scythed wagons (designed by Cyrus himself), hundreds of trained camels, archer jockeys, an armor-clad infantry, and crenelated towers. With the entire army chanting, the organized infantry, marching quickly toward the enemy, had such a severe impression on the frontline soldiers that they chose to run away, rather than stay and fight. The camels also impressed the horses, which threw their riders and fled.

Another problem for Croesus was, when he realized that many of his soldiers did not speak the same language and could not understand each other. Unlike Cyrus's camp, there was no organization or coordination enforced by the generals, and chaos was not avoidable.

Cyrus was actively involved at every corner of the war—riding his wagon, encouraging his loyal soldiers. When he witnessed the signs of chaos among the enemy soldiers, he stopped at the center of the camp and gave the good news to his generals and soldiers that they were on the verge of victory.

Croesus—at the center of the war, facing scythed wagons and the attacking camels—realized that he had no chance of success.

According to Herodotus, the Egyptian and the Babylonian soldiers had joined the Croesus's fighting forces, and the Egyptians, especially, were becoming effective on the left side of the battle. Cyrus hauled his army to the left, facing the brave Egyptian soldiers.

When Cyrus saw his army slaughtering the brave soldiers, he ordered them to stop the massacre. The Egyptian soldiers marveled at this noble gesture and made them convert and join Cyrus in the war.

The enemy was on the verge of defeat, and injudicious Croesus realized that the end was near, so he quickly began to retreat. The winter was approaching, and Croesus preferred to return to Sardis to wait for spring before regrouping.

Cyrus noted a sudden withdrawal of the enemy soldiers, and he noted that Croesus was leaving the devastated Pteria behind for him to take care of. The Persian king knew that he must follow with the battle until he brought the enemy into submission. Therefore, the war would not have any meaningful result. Despite knowing this fact, Cyrus gave Croesus a chance to reach Sardis, safe and secure, next to his family.

Cyrus sent a messenger to the Egyptian soldiers in his camp and asked them if they wanted to continue with him or to go home. He also said that after the war, they would be compensated, and they would have a choice then to return to Egypt or to stay wherever they would desire. The soldiers entirely accepted Cyrus's offer and stayed with him for the battle to come.

The Final Battle and Defeating Croesus at Lydia

As Croesus withdrew his army, he thought about a great comeback in springtime and projected a deadly attack. He spoke with his generals about reinforcing his army by hiring more soldiers from Greece and Sparta.

He was thinking that with the cold winter weather and such a long distance to travel, Cyrus would not be able to continue. It would be extremely difficult to carry all the wagons and soldiers across to Sardis, he thought. However, he underestimated Cyrus's persistence.

Croesus did not know that Cyrus was on his way and that he already was approaching Sardis in his wagon, along with the camels, scythed wagons, infantry, archers, and entire force.

Shortly thereafter, Cyrus arrived at the border of Sardis. He retired his entire military personnel in a large vacant area just outside of Sardis, expecting Croesus to make his move.

It was not long before Croesus lined up his cavaliers, archers, and all his forces. Soon after, the battle began, and it went on for a while, unsettled. Harpagus suggested using the camels against the enemy's cavaliers. According to Herodotus, the Greek historian, "Horses cannot stand the smell of camels, and they hate to be around them"; the horses ran away, dropping their riders.

Despite this predicament and discouraging outcome, Croesus continued with the fight, thoroughly using all his resources. There was no hope as he tumbled and gave up. His soldiers took refuge behind the city walls and citadels, leaving Cyrus and his army outside of the walls and its great heavy gate.

Herodotus said, at first, Cyrus continued fighting to enter the city, but his attempt was unsuccessful. His army remained behind the gate and walls—"kingdom wall"—under heavy surveillance from its towers and ramparts.

Fourteen days passed. Cyrus was still waiting for a breakthrough. He promised a reward to anyone who could find a way to enter the city. The next day, a guard named Haropas saw the helmet of a guarding soldier had fallen over the city wall, and the soldier promptly came down from a secret passageway, picked it up, and returned to the city. Anxiously, Haropas looked around and found the secret passage. Then he ran back to the camp and reported it to his general.

Cyrus was looking for that exact breakthrough. Soon after, the Aryan soldiers climbed up and entered the city. The soldiers then were able to open the heavy gate, and when the guarding soldiers saw that Cyrus's soldiers were entering the city, they fearfully ran away. By their running away, a disorder took over the city, and everybody ran to save his or her own life. Croesus also ran away and locked himself in his palace.

This victory came on a cold winter day, just before Cyrus's birthday in 546 BC.

Engraving of Cyrus Entering Sardis with Cassandane Standing Behind

Triumphant Speech

Cyrus, surrounded by his joyful generals and soldiers, unlike any other conquerors, delivered his peaceful victory speech.

"Praise is to the Lord, for without his will, this triumph would not have been possible. I assure the safety of the entire city. I promise that everybody in this city will be covered with an outstanding, enforced security. I am grateful to my brave soldiers and generals for their overwhelming suffering in the hot and cold weather, their hunger and thirst, their being a long way from their homes and families, and most of all, their bravery."

Warning: Soldiers to Respect the Civilians and Their Belongings

Some examples of the actions toward defeated nations by leaders prior to Cyrus explains the barbaric behaviors that existed in that era.

Nebuchadnezzar, after one of his victories, proudly wrote, "I ordered one hundred thousand eyes pulled out and one hundred thousand legs to be broken. With my own hands, I pulled out the commanders' eyes, and I burned one thousand boys and girls in fire; then destroyed their city so much that signs of life could not be found there."

Another example is from Sennacherib, the Assyrian king in 689 BC:

"When I conquered Babel, I took all people captive. I destroyed their houses and made them into a pile of dirt. I burned the entire city so bad that for days, the smoke went into the sky. I opened the water of the Tigris and the Euphrates toward the city, that the water even took away the remains of the destroyed city."

A statement made by Cyrus after victory in Sardis: "I have asked of the soldiers to respect all the people of the city, to respect their belongings and avoid looting the city."

Such a gesture was unusual for the citizens in Sardis because they had never heard that a conqueror could be so merciful. The standard at that time was to show the most violence toward defeated. Henceforth, the citizens of Sardis became comforted and returned to their daily lives

Historians and especially the holy books stated that Cyrus changed the violent behavior of humanity in the sixth century BC.

The Holy Bible inscribed his name as the savior of the humanity: "It was the will of God to protect him in his missions."

The citizens of Sardis watched, in surprise, every step that Cyrus took. Thus, the city was rejuvenated, delighted, and full of joy, and the people welcomed him with love.

Cyrus, accompanied by his friends and generals, walked around the overpopulated city. They noted that the city engaged in trade and businesses of various kinds. Retail stores, bath shops, barbershops, and residential complexes to accommodate tourists and travelers existed throughout the city. The business activities had gone unlike other cities, as the working class even prostituted their daughters. Farther away, the palace of Croesus was visible, surrounded by Cyrus's soldiers.

After Cyrus's victory, the Greeks wanted to sign a peace agreement, but this request was insulting to Cyrus—when he had asked them before the war, they refused to accept his offer. Therefore, Cyrus sent them a story in response to their request:

"A flute player saw a fish in the water, and he began playing a song so that maybe the fish would come out, but there was no result. Then he threw his net and caught many fish. Speaking to the fish, which were jumping up and down, he said, 'Now your dance is useless because when I was playing the flute you did not dance.'"

Friendly Behavior of Cyrus with Croesus

When Cyrus entered the palace, he found Croesus with fifteen of his loyal friends, gathered in the admitting area of the palace. One said, "Follow our everlasting tradition, and burn us in the burning fire outside."

The burning fire was at the center of the city, and an audience was gathered around, waiting for the tradition to take place.

Cyrus was profoundly affected and dispirited by such a request. He told Croesus, "I am not here to carry on such an inhumane and outrageous request and last wish."

Croesus insisted, but Cyrus rejected the tradition.

Outside the palace, the audience wondered when this sad and tragic event would occur. The awaiting audience suddenly saw Cyrus exit the palace. He announced that the burning fire was not necessary; there would not be any burning of any kind. This manly gesture of kindness brought joy to the public, and they began dancing in the rain, which was on its way.

With the help of a translator, Cyrus asked Croesus, "Who

suggested to you that you should enter my country? You could have stayed away and had me as a friend."

Croesus replied, "My bad fortune and your good luck caused my defeat and your victory. The Spartan's god Apollo encouraged me for this war. Otherwise, a person would be out of his mind to prefer war to peace, where fathers bury their sons instead of sons burying their fathers. What can I do? This is what gods wanted."

Cyrus asked Croesus for the reason of his suicidal wish.

"I wished to give my life to the fire in order to extinguish every god's anger. However, you stopped this process. Now I have to change my mind." Croesus remembered the words of his Greek friend Solon: "A person who would have glory and wealth at the end of life is a most prosperous person."

When Croesus noted the sincerity, honesty, and truthfulness, without tyrannical gestures, in Cyrus's behavior, he became illuminated and delighted, without worry and without fear.

They sat down and talked. Cyrus expressed that he was not happy to see that families were prostituting their daughters to strangers for the sake of money. He did not like to see believers believing in various Greek goddesses, while the city was the center for prostitutes. He did not like to see that fathers were sexually abusing their daughters. He did not like to see that everybody was focusing on obtaining only gold, silver, and wealth. He expressed his belief in the oneness of God and his rejection of worshiping the goddesses of the Greeks.

Croesus provided Cyrus with a detailed list of his kingdom's treasury and told him, "If you keep this list, you will know exactly what is there all the time. Therefore you can distinguish the honest from the dishonest guards."

Cyrus refused to look at it and gave the list to a confidant.

Surprised, Croesus told Cyrus that the treasury had rare and one-of-a-kind valuable jewels, gold, silver, and stones and that he should pay more attention to it.

Cyrus replied, "In your opinion, how much gold and silver would I have in all my kingdom if I would have acted as you advised?"

Croesus called a significantly high number.

Cyrus replied, "Very well. Now send someone you really trust with my cousin Vishtasb and go among my friends. Tell them that I need money; then write down the total amount in detail; then bring it to me."

Croesus did not take the matter seriously, but he did what Cyrus asked of him. When the amount was tallied and revealed to Cyrus, he said that, in his opinion, the amount was much higher than what he had estimated.

When Cyrus saw the look of marvel on Croesus's face, he said, "You see, Croesus, I have such a treasury. You suggested that I keep the gold and jewels in my kingdom for myself so my friends and my confidants would become jealous and envious of me. I'd have to hire trusted guards to keep them safe. I have my own way. I make my friends rich, and they have to keep their wealth safe. They are my treasures and treasury. This way, they serve me with honestly." Cyrus looked at Croesus. "I would like to tell you another point—I do not argue. I do not wish to bury treasure underground or keep it in a treasury bank. I spend it for my friends. If I had more, I would not be able to eat or drink more."

Social Reform; Leaving Lydia for Persia with Croesus and His Family

It was time for the soldiers and Cyrus to return to Persia. At this point, Cyrus had expanded his empire to be the largest ever. He selected soldiers from Lydia who wanted to join his forces and discharged those who did not wish to serve. He remained in Sardis into spring. Then, it was much easier to move his large military back home.

In addition to all his military personnel, he respectfully invited Croesus and his family to go with him to live in Iran.

Thereafter, Cyrus became aware of a need to modify the lifestyle in Sardis in order to respect family laws and believe in one God. He appointed Tabalos as a new leader to implement these corrections. However, after a short while, the residents of Sardis revolted. The uprising was led by Pactyas, a government treasury guard, and Tabalos could not bring it to a peaceful conclusion. Croesus suggested that it was not wise to go against the people of the city but only to focus on punishing Pactyas.

Cyrus sent a small force, commanded by Mazares to instill order in Sardis. Mazares was also to disarm the people of Lydia. As soon as Pactyas heard that Cyrus's forces were on the way, he escaped to Chios Island, but people arrested him and exchanged him for a tax-free ownership of their island. The Aryan bases in

Lydia were established, and slowly, people adapted to the new conditions and the lifestyle.

Mazares, after establishing order in Sardis, brought several additional Greek colonies under the Persian Empire. Thereafter, due to a severe illness, Mazares passed away, and Cyrus appointed the Median general Harpagus to replace him.

Harpagus constructed hills, fronting walls around some Greek cities. Hence, the people of Phocaea (the largest Greek city after Miletus), instead of surrendering, ran away and took refuge somewhere in Italy. It became easy for Harpagus to immediately possess new territories. Therefore, the Aryans had conquered the widest geographical territories under a Persian king.

The Greeks and the people of Asia Minor, in addition to paying more than Croesus's reign tax, were required to compensate for their security by having the Persian military guard their cities.

Cyrus did not interfere with the daily affairs of the Greeks, but he knew that in case of a war, he could use the Greek ships in the battle zone.

After the War, Spending His Time with Aryan Tribes

After the affairs in Lydia and conquering additional territories in Asia Minor, Cyrus instructed his generals to govern and attend to all matters, such as peacekeeping, finances, tax collection, and so forth. They banded together to make a report in a specific timeframe.

For six years, Cyrus was free from war engagements with great nations. During this time, he focused on strengthening his northeast borders. In this process, he added territories, such as parts of Afghanistan, parts of India, parts of Pakistan, Khwarazm, Khorasan, Sistan, and, from the northwest, Caucasia and Armenia into his empire.

Cyrus took the time to construct buildings in Pasargadae, the Persian capital, and in his grandfather's Median capital city of Ecbatana.

The most important of all was to reach his desire, which he never had a chance to do because of Croesus's attack. This desire was to spend time with different tribes—the Derousiaioi, the Medes, the Persians, the Sagartians, and all residents of the Iranian plateau who called themselves the Aryans.

An interesting encounter during these six years for Cyrus and his military happened far in the east, where they found people naked and living in primitive conditions. The tribe was living so far from civilization that when they saw a huge army and received Cyrus's unselfish generosity, they were astonished. They learned about Cyrus, the Persians, and their culture. They volunteered to become part of Cyrus's empire. Though they were not his beneficiaries, Cyrus pledged to provide them with education and safety. This gesture encouraged their neighboring tribes to do the same.

On the way back, Cyrus conquered an Aryan tribe that was occupying part of India. Cyrus then realized that from every corner, his empire was secure, and no territory could be a menace.

He realized that his political system was without a threat from anyone and was working well. He realized that his generals and his governors in every corner of the world were protecting his realm.

He realized that there were economic advancements, people had jobs, and they loved his character and cherished his fairness.

What makes people willingly obey some rulers but not others? He thanked God for giving him directions and guiding him through, helping him to carry out fairness, and achieve his accomplishments.

At home, he spent time in Pasargadae's garden, located in the middle of an agricultural field. The garden was full of trees, flowers, and beautiful green grass, often cared for by Cyrus himself.

Xenophon, the Greek historian, quoted a Spartan general, as saying, "We were walking through the garden, organized perfectly. All flowers were at the same level, and the fragrance in the garden fascinated me. I opened my mouth to praise, a thousand times, the gardener. Cyrus responded, 'The trees that you see—I grew them by my hands. Every time that I am away from battles, I come here and sow before dinner.'"

The irrigation water flowed in a stream that was divided from a river near the palace. Cyrus had made the division and had constructed a bridge over it.

Persia/Iran

Before I continue with the rest of the story, it is important to clarify the confusing name change of Persia to Iran that is so unclear for many around the world. I have an extended discussion in A Basket of Goodies, page 85, about this matter and here are parts for clarification. "Perhaps, one of the most misspelled, misrepresented names in the world is the name Iran." The book furthermore explains how the name was misspelled. "Iran as is spelled in English does not represent what the name was originally changed to mean. The reason the ancient name *Persia* was changed to the modern *Iran* is because it has come to light that at the beginning of the second millennium BCE, the ancestors of the Aryans settled in the land today called Iran. The Aryans were a broad population, including the Medes and the Persians. Tribes each occupied a different part of Iran. Thus, the name Iran was adapted to signify and represent the land that was occupied by the Aryans." The book explains how the name in Farsi (Iranian language) sounds fine but in the English does not, "...the spelling of the English version should reflect the intent; it could be Aran or Aryan or some other form, but not Iran. However, nobody is at fault but those early translators that did not know what they were doing and brought this mass of confusion into a great nation's history.

It is also essential to note that Persia always had larger territories than Iran today. For example, most southern countries released from the Russian Communism that are neighboring the Caspian Sea belonged to Persia. Countries such as Kazakhstan, Tajikistan, Turkmenistan, Uzbekistan, located on the east side of the sea and most areas called Caucasus, located on the west side of the sea, as well as the Caspian Sea were all lost to Russia in the 19th century by two treaties, Turkmenchay and Gulistan.

The rivalry between the Arabs and the Persians is not only because the Arabs invaded Persia and interrupted their way of life, but because during the invasion, speaking Persian was prohibited and tongues were pulled out if one spoke Persian. That is the reason why the Persian scientists in math, medicine, physics, philosophy, and astrology wrote their findings in Arabic causing flourish of the Islamic Golden Age, particularly during the reign of the Abbasid caliph Harun al Rashid.

The Persian language was saved by the bravery of poet Firdausi, who despite of a dangerous condition wrote his poems in Persian. Other poets followed him and kept the language alive such as Omar Khayyam, Attar, Rumi, Sadie, Hafiz and many others. An Egyptian friend once said, "If we had a Firdausi in our country, we would be speaking our own language too today, instead of speaking Arabic."

It is also important to mention that even the Ottoman Empire came from the Persians and were offspring of the Persian Turkish Dynasties in Persia during the 11th and 12th centuries and thereafter. These dynasties are the Ghaznavid, Seljuks, Timurid, and Safavids to the latest Qajars.

The Persians were skillful in storytelling. Some of their everlasting stories revealed in A Basket of Goodies are, *Lila and Majnoon, Sinbad the Sailor, Kalylo Damneh,* and the most entertaining of all, *One Thousand and One Nights. Nights* contains series of stories told by Scheherazade (Shahrzad) to her captive king and husband, Shahryar to prevent her death. It has the stories such as *Aladdin and the Magic Lamp*, the animated and copyrighted Disney movie story, which its origin was never revealed, *Ali Baba and the Forty Thieves* and so on. *Nights* was converted to Arabic by Caliph Harun al Rashid with a new name, *Arabian Nights. Nights* has been translated to virtually every major language of the world in the modern time.

I hope this briefing of history offer a perspective and change readers' view about a country called, Iran today.

Now, here is the rest of the story of Cyrus the Great.

CHAPTER 4

Babylon, a Great Civilization

If Babylon is not the oldest civilization, it can be considered as one of the oldest. According to historians, its first dynasty traced back to 1830–1531 BC.

Babylon was the center of science and, from time to time, held the premiere scientific center of the ancient world. Astronomy, medicine, philosophy, arithmetic, and geography were subjects in their studies. The emphasis was on astronomy, but the purpose was directed toward the measurement of the seven heavens and the twelve signs of the zodiac. Astrologers did not look at stars for their scientific value but to fulfill their overwhelming superstitious beliefs.

Excessive superstitious beliefs created an environment for prostitution and idolatry, where young girls believed they must go to the temple of Aphrodite and sleep with strangers for a coin in order to complete their sacred mission.

Married women also had their strange manners in dinner gatherings, believing in the sacred prostitution, rewarded by the fertility goddess Ishtar. This intricate submission effectively coerced young girls' minds from childhood and became part of their beliefs and, hence, their behaviors.

Young girls thoroughly believed in the necessity and the sacredness of the process so that they gave themselves to the temple before they could marry. They believed deeply in magic and witchcraft throughout their lives.

There are many stories regarding this intricate submission, such as *The Egyptian*, a magnum opus written by Mika Waltari (1908–1979), which is a great example of the lifestyle of the time. The main character Sinuhe, the pharaoh's physician, had a chance to travel. He involved himself with a girl who needed to give herself to the temple.

In those days, Babylon had a dike between the Tigris and the Euphrates Rivers, with a ditch deep outside of the rivers to render difficulties to the cavalries of the enemy. Defensive reinforcements made it impossible to attack Babylon, and that was the reason that it remained safe for centuries.

After Nebuchadnezzar's death, there was political chaos, rooted in the differences between the two oldest tribes, the Kaldani and the Arami. Another social dilemma arose among army generals and the clergy. For this reason, in six short years, three kings came to power, and because of the unrest, one after another failed. Finally, after six years, the sixty-five-year-old Nabonidus came to power and became the king.

Historians do not have much information about his life; he became a mysterious character in history. Nevertheless, his father was said to be one of the Arami tribe and a leading man in

Babylon. Nabonidus himself claimed that he was not from a kingdom family, but it was only by goddess will that he became the king.

During the forty-three years that Nebuchadnezzar reigned, Babylon reached its zenith and became the most powerful nation of the time. His father, Nabopolassar, felt threatened by the Egyptian pharaoh, so he sent his son to battle their aggression. The Egyptians were defeated and lost Syria as well as Palestine, and the Babylonian Empire was extended, bordering Egypt.

Nebuchadnezzar conquered Jerusalem and destroyed houses so badly that nobody remained alive. He carried on, taking the Jews into captivity, including the prophet Daniel. While he was on his Jerusalem mission, he heard that his father had died. He rushed back to Babylon to announce his kingdom, but because he had no chance to bring the captives, he ordered to carry on as planned. He attacked three times, thereafter destroying temples and houses, and he brought all the captured Jews to Babylon. During these raids and nonstop tyranny, he demolished temple of Solomon, burned houses and buildings, destroyed the walls, and killed religious leaders and many people. At last, he brought back fifteen thousand executives, businesspersons, artists, leaders, and children of prophets, with their gold, silver, priceless jewels, and their belongings.

Nebuchadnezzar was a troubled character, but during his reign in Babylon, he made great constructions and many improvements. It was also a clever choice to marry Amytis, a Median noble family's daughter; thus, he could maintain a peaceful relationship with the Medes.

Historians mention that he built the Hanging Gardens of Babylon, one of the seven wonders of the ancient world, when Amytis was homesick, to remind her of the green maintained in her homeland in northwest Iran. During Nebuchadnezzar's forty-three-year reign, he finished the construction of many temples, some of which had taken three hundred years to build, such as the temple of sky and earth, the Tower of Babylon, and a ziggurat. As Herodotus said, temples were uniquely finished with a gold chair and a beautifully designed carpet. The Marduk temple was so shining that it was called the "Shining of the Sun."

The Bible has stated that at the end of his atrocious life, Nebuchadnezzar became insane, and his lunacy made him think that he was a cow, living in the forest, and his wife was the ruler of Babylon. However, this is only a story and does not have documented proof by the historians.

Over the years, Babylon became extremely wealthy, especially after the fall of Lydia. Traders from Greece, Egypt, Lydia, and Asia Minor went there for business, either to purchase merchandise or to sell products directly to consumers or dealers.

The geographical position of Babylon created a great trading market. It could be reached from three continents—Asia, Africa and Europe—either by land access or by sea—the Red Sea from the west and the Persian Gulf from east.

After fall of the Medes, with whom the Babylonians had a friendly relationship, Babylon became uneasy and reinforced its borders against any intruding forces. However, the corruption within and holding fifty thousand Jewish prisoners made this overwhelmingly rich nation an unhappy place for many to live in.

The city was surrounded with walls, erected three hundred feet high and seventy-five feet wide. Some of these walls were made by Nebuchadnezzar, as well as deep ditches around the walls to protect the city further. These walls had one hundred metal gates decorated with colorful tiles.

Turmoil in Babylon after Nebuchadnezzar's Death

Babylon was the most important city in the world, with a population of two hundred thousand people. The Tower of Babylon took three hundred years to build, and its construction was completed during Nebuchadnezzar's reign. It was seven floors high, with one floor underground. It was the second tallest building in the world, after the Great Pyramid in Egypt.

The Euphrates passed through the middle of the city. The entrance and the exit of the river was constructed strongly of bricks, which made it impossible to penetrate. A bridge over the river connected both sides of the city, which naturally was divided into two sections. One section held the palace and the Hanging Gardens; the other side held the holy temples, such as Marduk and the Tower of Babel, dedicated to Marduk, which was believed to be erected between heaven and earth. It was three hundred feet wide, facing the earth, and three hundred feet high, facing the sky. The Tigris was another river that irrigated Babylon's agricultural lands

Ritual prostitution was not limited to Babylon, as the Lydians and the Greeks also practiced this ritual. However, fingers often pointed toward Babylon but not toward other countries.

Nabonidus was not from a kingdom family, as he repeatedly indicated. He was not from the military generals either and therefore was not trained to be a king. This lack of experience caused political chaos and social unrest in Babylon.

Another issue with Nabonidus was his personal belief. Even though he worshipped the Babylonian gods Marduk, Nabu, Nargol, and Shamash, he also worshipped Sīn, not a traditional Babylonian god. He tried hard to reform the Babylonians' beliefs, either to replace Marduk with Sīn or to influence them toward accepting Sīn. This introduction caused tensions to rise and to increase the public's disapproval. At the time that he had occupied himself with the reform, he left the country in the hands of his son Belshazzar, which created a further dilemma for the regime.

Nabonidus was interested in collecting antiques and old idols from other nations. Bringing other nations' idols into Babylon caused an uncomfortable feeling among the average citizens, especially the clergy.

The Jewish prisoners, who had lived in captivity for almost seventy years, were waiting for their savior, as had been prophesied, and that brought hope among the prisoners that the promised time was near. The clergy, the captive prisoners, and the average people were waiting for a person to save them from this calamity and suffering.

Finally, this prophecy in the world, with its anticipation, came to reality.

Cyrus's Quest for Justice behind the Walls of Babylon

As historians have agreed, Cyrus never meant to collect wealth for himself on his missions but to campaign against tyranny and to establish justice, dividing the wealth among all. This noble idea of justice for all was always behind his ethical standards, motivating him to achieve his main purpose.

It was impossible to penetrate Babylon's walls. As Herodotus said, these wonder walls blocked the city further, with five deep ditches providing more protection. The two rivers, Tigris and Euphrates, were secured at their points of entrance and exit with bricks, providing further defense for the city.

Though Babylon was the finest country and well protected at the time, it declined due to its lack of moral standards, idol worshiping, superstitious beliefs, ritual prostitution, witchcraft practices, and other complex social unrest. Consequently, it became an easy target for Cyrus, well known for his kindness and social-structure reforms, to follow with his mission to become the favorite leader in Babylon.

Historians have different views of how this victory came about, however, and despite the secured strong walls and deep ditches, Cyrus found a way to succeed without much bloodshed.

After the necessary preparation, Cyrus decided that it was time to take Babylon into his kingdom. According to Herodotus, when Cyrus was crossing the Karkheh River, the water level was so high that it took away his favorite white horse. This incident made him so upset that he pledged to reduce the water level so women could cross without tearing their garments. For this purpose, soldiers made thirty-six streams that inverted the water flow in those streams. It took all the summer to carry out this mission, so Cyrus postponed his journey for six months.

Historians are convinced that by directing the water into different streams, Cyrus began agricultural improvement in these deserted areas, even before the fall of Babylon.

Although Babylon's territories were limited, over the years, it had extended it territory to Syria, Jerusalem, Mesopotamia, and parts of the Arabian island. They became friendly with the Egyptians, their old enemy, in order to combine forces against Cyrus, but Amasis, the pharaoh of Egypt, refused to cooperate.

Cyrus was near Babylon with his army, where a minor war was triggered. It was brief, and the Babylonian soldiers quickly escaped and took a refuge behind the walls, where people had food and necessities that would last them for a year. They did not worry if their city was besieged. Nabonidus also did not worry, thinking that eventually, Cyrus would run out of food, his soldiers would be tired, and they would give up and return to Iran. The enforced gates and surrounding walls would not allow any desperate actions.

After all, his son, Belshazzar, was in charge of the affairs, more so than the real king, who was busy with his old idols collection. It just happened that in those days, Belshazzar had a large festival, which the Greeks and the Jews historically referred to as the Great Banquet of Babylon. While happy and joyful with their entertainment, they were dismissively laughing and mocking the Persian army behind the walls. They would say, "Behind the walls and under the sun's rays, they will annihilate."

While Belshazzar was drinking and in a joyful mood,

surrounded by his wives, he ordered that the gold and silver plates and cups be brought from Jerusalem for their pleasure.

Writings on the Wall and Their Meanings

They were busy gratifying themselves and drinking wine when suddenly, according to the Holy Scriptures, a hand appeared and, next to the candle holder, wrote this phrase: Mene, Tekel, Peres.

Belshazzar became uncomfortable and worried. He summoned his interpreters, witches, and conjurers and told them, "If any of you can understand and explain to me the meaning of these words on the wall, I will give that person a gold necklace; hence, a job as the third governor."

All the gathered conjurers looked at the words, one at a time, but none could understand the secret writing.

While unsettled Belshazzar was worrying, the queen entered, wished him a long and prosperous life, and said, "In our country, there is a person who has a godly spirit. His illumine appeared in your father's presence, and your father appointed him to be in charge of magicians and astrologers. His name is Daniel; he is a Jewish prisoner and famous for interpreting dreams. He is the only one who can help you."

Belshazzar immediately ordered that Daniel be brought to him, and when he was brought forth, Belshazzar asked, "Are you the same Jewish Daniel who was brought here from Jerusalem?" Without hesitation, he then commanded, "Interpret the writings on the wall so I can reward you generously."

Daniel replied, "Keep your generosity to yourself, and give

your reward to another person. However, I will read and explain what the words on the wall mean. The God that solely belongs to him, and he is the Almighty, who sent the hand to write these words, which, word by word, bear the following meanings. *Mene* means that your kingdom is just about to end; *tekel* means that your kingdom will fall into flaws; and *peres* means that your kingdom is divided between the Medes and the Persians."

As it appears in the Bible,

> Then from his presence, the hand was sent, and this writing was inscribed. And this is the writing that was inscribed MENE, MENE, TEKEL, and PARSIN. This is the interpretation of the matter: MENE, God has numbered the days of your kingdom and brought it to an end; *TEKEL, you have been weighed in* the balances and found wanting; PERES, your kingdom is divided and given to the Medes and Persians. (Daniel 5:24–28)

Belshazzar did not take Daniel's interpretation seriously, and thereafter, they continued with their celebration.

While there was a celebration inside the palace, Cyrus the Great was busy excavating a canal underground and diverting the flow of the water of the Tigris. Cyrus's work seemed useless to the people inside the palace. They said that the men were busy with an unsuccessful task and they mocked and laughed. Occasionally, they came out to see if the erected walls were holding strong, but then they would go back and continue with their entertainment.

This optimism made them pledge donations to their favorite temple.

The soldiers, however, were working expeditiously to divert the flow of water, while Cyrus and Gobryas, the former governor of Susa, a Babylonian, who had joined Cyrus, watched closely. Cyrus was a warrior and a man with tremendous planning and vision; he had superb mind power to overcome any obstacles.

One day, the people woke up and did not see any signs of the besieging soldiers outside the walls. They thought that they had gathered and left during the night. It was at that time when Belshazzar's celebration extended outside the palace, with people's participation in dancing and singing.

Cyrus assigned Gobryas, the former governor of Susa, to lead the Aryan army. From the time that he joined the army, he learned much about their customs and culture, and he found out that it was imperative to respect other peoples' rights; to consider saying a prayer before eating; to try to be humorous and funny without mocking anyone; and to avoid an infuriating manner at all times.

Cyrus was looking at the soldiers and the complex and complicated work that was needed to divert the water flow of the Tigris. Such a project needed great conviction. Compared with even today's technology, it seems like an extremely difficult task.

Triumph of Cyrus in Babylon

On that final night, the water level was so much reduced that soldiers were able to walk inside the city, where people were busy dancing and pleasing themselves. They found out that the guards also were singing and participating in the entertainment activities, leaving the security of the city unattended.

Suddenly, it became known that the city had fallen to Cyrus's army, and Babylon was conquered.

People were in shock that the main gate of the city was opened and that Cyrus the Great was walking straight into the palace, accompanied by Gobryas and his generals, without any bloodshed.

In a few short hours, which the prophet Daniel had anticipated, the noises outside the palace brought a silence to the banquet. It was the grinding sound of the special guards, protecting the palace.

The large door of palace opened, and Cyrus and his generals entered the banquet. Astonished, Belshazzar wondered what he needed to do. The participants became determined to continue with their entertainment—appalling, as it was too late for the banquet. Belshazzar took out his sword and fought Gobryas, and that's when the future king of Babylon received his deadly strike.

This political phenomenon became real in 539 BC. Despite all its economic resources, military power, and secured walls, it was in this way that Cyrus the Great conquered Babylon.

Though it was impossible to penetrate the walls, Cyrus had assessed that the only way to enter Babylon was through the Tigris River's canal.

Herodotus stated, "When the direction of the water diverted to give an entranceway to the soldiers, Babylon, including its security soldiers and guards, were asleep, and that made it easier for Cyrus's soldiers to conquer the city. They controlled the city before dawn and before people were awake."

The city, by the standards of those days, was rather a large city, with a population of two hundred thousand people. This mission was accomplished so quickly that many people were not aware of it, even the next day.

By the order of Cyrus, soldiers maintained their utmost respect for the residents of Babylon. They did not rob the treasury temples, nor did they rob individuals, despite the customary manner of all previous conquerors.

Social Justice and Reform in Babylon

Soon, the Babylonians noticed Cyrus's magnanimity and ethical behavior. They noted that their temples were safe, and they had not been harmed or robbed. Crowds of people came to see him, throwing flowers at his feet and welcoming him to their city. They believed that Cyrus was sent by the gods to take away the tyranny, injustice, and suppression put on them by Nabonidus.

The people loathed Nabonidus because of his abominable deeds and for various other reasons—he interfered with their beliefs, did not attend to the necessities of political affairs, and did not attend their annual festival. He also had two other major predicaments: he left his reign in the hands of his pleasure-seeking son, and the captive Jewish people were kept as either slaves or as prisoners as they waited for the fulfillment of their prophecy.

Cyrus the Great knew that, at first, he must bring peace to various ecclesiastic sectors. Cyrus wanted to prove that he would protect Babylon and that there would be no menace thereafter. He walked through the city, visiting different areas; in particular, he wanted to see the temples that were beloved by the public.

Historians have stated that Cyrus, at that time, ordered the return of the gods that Nabonidus had sent away, to be placed in their primary temples. He also commanded that all people were free to worship any god that they wished to worship.

Babylonians believed that Marduk, the great god, had raised Cyrus to provide justice for all people.

"He should to be the king of all kings," they said. They believed that Marduk, the great god and protector of all the people in Babylon, knew of Cyrus's good deeds and pure heart and that he had sent Cyrus, showed him the road, walked with him side by side, and provided him with the means to conquer Babylon without a battle. The infidel king Nabonidus was then in Cyrus's hands, to do as he desired with him. Hence, the governors and wise men bowed their heads in front of him and were thereafter loyal to his kingdom.

Cyrus again went to the temple, honored Marduk, and participated in the ceremony, accompanied by his wife and Cambyses, his son. With his presence, Cyrus induced the clergy as well as the public to accept his leadership and to be loyal to him and his son.

Though Cyrus believed in the oneness of God, he did not impose his beliefs upon the people in Babylon. He ordered his clerk to write a declaration of his political view toward religion:

"All humankind is created equal, and everyone is free to worship as they feel suited."

Thus, the first declaration of human rights came into existence in 538 BC.

The conquest of Babylon on October 12, 539 BC, was a significant step toward recognition of equality, freedom, and the establishment of human rights. It was an achievement, especially, for the freedom of choice in religion, extending throughout millennia, even to today.

Cyrus's victory, instead of being a massacre and historical disappointment, brought joy and happiness to the people of Babylon. People of every nation under Cyrus's realm realized that there was progress, freedom, fairness, and justice for all.

Cyrus appointed Gobryas to be the governor in Babylon and ordered a condolence ceremony for Belshazzar. He ordered his generals to keep order for as long as they stayed in the city, to look after people's wealth and dignity without interruption, and to ensure that different professions—teachers teach, traders trade, and every sector of the society—would keep their jobs without any economic downside.

In order to avoid any sort of future revolt, Cyrus sent Nabonidus to live in Kerman, Iran, where later he had a position as the governor.

Croesus wrote, "After the triumph in Babylon, Cyrus ordered his soldiers and generals to avoid robbing and to avoid looting the city. Therefore and for this reason, Babylonians dearly loved Cyrus."

Historians believe that one of the major causes of social unrest in Babylon was that Nabonidus, in his seventeen-year reign, did not spend much time in Babylon, nor did he participate in the customary New Year's festival, which required the king's attendance; therefore, the festival was not in vogue for a few years.

Every day, Cyrus appeared front of gods with food in his hands—the same gods that he had ordered brought back, as well as any others. This action brought further joy to the hearts of the people. Cyrus cut the influence of military men from the temples and returned the work of the temples to the clergy. Marduk, the grand god protector of the people, became happy and directed Cyrus to correct wrongdoings of Nabonidus, who did not believe in him.

Shortly after his governorship appointment, Gobryas died of old age, and a Babylonian noble name Nabu-ahhe-bullit was chosen by Cyrus to replace him.

Cyrus, in an inscription found in an ancient temple named Eanna, proclaimed,

"I am Cyrus ... My ... soldiers entered peacefully in Babylon, and I did not let anybody frighten anyone .... I established peace in Babel and other cities. I freed people from [the] yoke, which they engaged. I returned comforts into agitated and disturbed houses, ended tragedy in their lives, and ended their disastrous conditions. Marduk the grand god came to illuminate my deeds and bestowed me with his grace."

After the victory in Babylon, Cyrus focused forcefully on maintaining unity among all sectors to retain its identity in the form of social economy, to avoid any changes, and, most of all, to render social justice in Babylon. Therefore, people remained in their jobs and in their positions, and no price increase was applied to products, especially primary products relating to food. He focused on maintaining an unchanged economy so it could reach an improved condition.

One of the elite sectors of society was the clergy, which found an opportunity to renew its old tradition, met by Cyrus's protection and his empowerment.

While Cyrus occupied himself with the affairs in Babylon, his beloved wife, Cassandane, died. There was a public mourning for five days, from March 21 until March 26. Cassandane had accompanied Cyrus in all wars and she was mother of the prince, Cambyses.

Over the years, particularly after the war with the Egyptians, Babylon's territories had extended to Syria and Palestine and bordered Egypt. Consequently, after his victory in Babylon, the territories covered under Cyrus expanded to vast parts of the world, creating an empire that never had existed before.

In order to participate in economic opportunities, all western realms volunteered to join the Persian. Therefore, businessmen in Asia Minor, Lydia, Babylon, Media, Persia, and everywhere were happy to see a large government that would protect them and provide them a safer environment, as well as international roads.

Tower of Babylon

Freedom of Captive Jews in Babylon

Perhaps Cyrus's most important accomplishment in Babylon was the declaration of freedom. By establishing this law, he was able to free the Hebrews from their captivity. The Bible indicates that Cyrus was a kind person; in addition, it mentions that his kindness was further toward the Jewish tribe. It also describes how this historic tragedy accorded. Even though historians do not refer to the Bible as a dependable source of history, many historical points are shared between the words of the Bible and the words of historians.

The Bible indicates that at the end of the seven century BC, the Jews became corrupted, diverting their beliefs to idol worshiping and forgetting the idea of the oneness of God. Their prophets of the time guided them in the right direction, but they refused to accept. One of those prophets was Jeremiah, who warned them and even by hung heavy wood on his neck to demonstrate his body's reaction to it, to portray the Jews in Babylonian captivity. However, this demonstration did not work, and Jeremiah suffered disgrace, persecution, and imprisonment and eventually was exiled to Egypt.

Nebuchadnezzar besieged Jerusalem in the third or fourth year of the reign of Jehoiakim, the son of the king of Judah, and destroyed the temple of Solomon in 587–586 BC.

It is evident that this persecution and suffering lasted during all forty-three years of Nebuchadnezzar's reign and even for years after his death, for almost seventy years, until Cyrus was sent by God to terminate this imprisonment in 539 BC.

After victory, Cyrus ordered that the Jews be freed from captivity. He announced that the tribe could return to Jerusalem to take part in building the house of God. If one did not have the means to donate, Cyrus said others must help that person with their gold or silver or selling their animals until the temple was constructed. He ordered the rebuilding of the temple that Nebuchadnezzar had destroyed as well.

Babylon Captivity of the Jews (597-539BC)

Cyrus's work with the Hebrew tribe was not complete until he made an announcement, in a formal command, to take out goods and commodities from the treasury that Nebuchadnezzar had brought to Babylon from Jerusalem and give them to the Jewish guardians to return to Jerusalem. Historians believe these goods included sixty gold trace and cups; 1,410 silver trace and cups; and over one thousand other valuable commodities, which were all returned to their primary location, Jerusalem.

CHAPTER 5

Cyrus in the Holy Bible

It was indicative of righteousness that the deeds of the Hebrew tribe would induce their deserved punishment and that the forthcoming hardships would teach them the Word of God and the paths of his cabinet.

During their long captivity, tribulation, and tyranny, the window of hope remained always open, and the tribe knew that eventually, somehow, they would be freed from this captivity. Many prophets, such as Daniel, Ezra, Isaiah, and Jeremiah, have a named book in the Bible that describes their calamitous and jubilant times.

The book of Daniel speaks much of the faith and of encountering struggles during captivity. It can be difficult to follow, however, as the book of Daniel jumps from one king to another, without order. For example, chapter 5 is dedicated to the handwriting-on-the-wall incident, while chapter 6 is about Daniel in the lion's den, the story of his relationship with King Darius. King Darius became the king years after the writing-on-the-wall incident. What happen with all those years in between? How did Daniel end up in Iran with Darius? What happened to Cyrus? How did he become free? Despite one's logical mind, however, where there is a faith, there are no questions!

The Book of Daniel

> And you his son, Belshazzar, have not humbled your heart, though you knew all this. (Daniel 5:22)
>
> PERES, your kingdom is divided and given to the Medes and Persians. ... Then the King was exceedingly glad, and commanded that Daniel be taken up out the den. So Daniel was taken up out the den, and no kind of harm was found on him, because he had trusted in his God. And the king commanded, and those men had maliciously accused Daniel were brought and cast into the den of lion. (Daniel 5:28; 6:23–24)

The Book of Ezra

The book of Ezra consists of ten chapters. Chapters 1–6 relate to the period of Cyrus the Great and the dedication of the second temple.

> In the first years of Cyrus king of Persia, that the world of the LORD by the mouth of Jeremiah

might be fulfilled; the LORD stirred up the spirit of Cyrus king of Persia, so that he made a proclamation throughout all the kingdom and also put it in writing: Thus says Cyrus king of Persia: the LORD, the God of heaven, has given me all the kingdom of the earth, and he has charged me to build him a house at Jerusalem, which is in Judah. (Ezra 1:1–2)

So they gave money to the masons and the carpenters, and food, drink, and oil to the Sidonians and the Tyrians to bring cedar trees from Lebanon to the sea, to Joppa, according to the grant that they had from Cyrus king of Persia. (Ezra 3:7)

However, in first year of Cyrus the king of Persia of Babylon, Cyrus the king made decree that this house of God should be rebuilt. (Ezra 5:13)

And in Ecbatana, the citadel that is in the province of Media, a scroll was found on which this was written: A record. ... And the people of Israel, the priests and the Levites; and the rest of the returned exiles, celebrated the dedication of the house of God with joy. ... On the fourteenth day of the first month, the returned exiles kept the Passover. (Ezra 6:2, 16, 19)

The Book of Isaiah

Isaiah was the son of Amos, who was the first major prophet to have a book consisting of nine chapters. The book of Isaiah, however, contains sixty-six chapters and explains how God will make a royal savior and a Messiah rule Jerusalem—Cyrus the Great.

> Who stirred up one from the east whom victory meets at every step? He gives up nations before him, so that he tramples kings underfoot, he makes them like dust with his sword, like driven stubble with his bow. (Isaiah 41:2)
>
> Who says of Cyrus, He is my shepherd, and he shall fulfill all my purpose: Saying of Jerusalem, 'she shall be built,' and of the temple,' your foundation shall be laid. (Isaiah 44:28)
>
> Thus says the LORD to Cyrus, whose right hand I have grasped to subdue nations before him and to loose the belts of kings, to open doors before him that gates may not be closed. (Isaiah 45:1)
>
> Go through, go through the gates; prepare the way for the people; build up, build up the highway; clear it of stones; lift up a signal over the people. (Isaiah 62:10)

The Book of Jeremiah

> Will you steal, murder, commit adultery, swear falsely; make offering to Baal, and go after other Gods that you have not known. (Jeremiah 7:9)

> I set a snare for you and you were taken, O Babylon, and you did not know it; you were bound and caught, because you opposed the LORD. (Jeremiah 5:24)

> And the king of Babylon struck them down and put them to death at Riblah in the land of Hamath. So Judah was taken into exile out of his land. (Jeremiah 52:27)

After the conquest of Babylon by Cyrus the Great, the language of prophets mostly focused on rebuilding the faith, temples, and Jerusalem.

Was Cyrus the Will of God?

Cyrus concluded and carried out what was promised by the prophecies of the prophets—to free the captured prisoners. God made him to write a commandment and send it to his wide empire: "I am Cyrus, the Persian king, announcing that God, the God of the sky, who bestowed all these nations upon me, thereupon I can build the house of God in Jerusalem. Hereupon, I am asking all Jewish people living in my country to go there if they want to build this house of God."

Cyrus's respect for the Hebrew tribe caused many of them to migrate and to live in Iran. The trend lasted from generation to generation for thousands of years. Therefore, the Jews genuinely became Iranians, maybe as much as other ancient tribes did. One of those people who went to live in Iran was Daniel, the prophet, who stayed there for the rest of his life. Six burial cities claimed the tomb of Daniel was located in the territories of then-Persia (today's Iran), and the most famous of all is a site known as Shush-e Daniyal.

It is important to note that Cyrus's manifest was not as worthy for any other tribes as much as it was for the Jewish tribe. No other tribes from the ancient ages are so thankful and full of gratitude for the ethics applied by Cyrus the Great as is the Hebrew tribe.

Without a doubt, one would prefer to have these controversies than have nothing at all. Therefore, the source of all knowledge of ancient history, including this book, is the writings of the Greek historians.

Tomb of Cyrus in Pasargadae, Iran

CHAPTER 6

The Passing of Cyrus the Great

The eagles were flying high, the lions were roaring, the horses neighing, the monkeys mourning, and the birds singing their saddest songs, preparing the world for the death of its greatest ruler ever—a king who earned the title of King of Kings, a king who produced freedom of speech, a king who produced a declaration of human rights, and a king who introduced kindness, dignity, and morality among humankind.

As with the rule of the nature—that everything and everyone must die one day—the fruitful life of Cyrus also ended in the year 529 BC.

From being an unknown child in Ecbatana, living with a shepherd and his wife, to going to Pasargadae and becoming the greatest leader is all the story of Cyrus the Great.

According to the narrative composed by Xenophon, the Greek physician and the historian, Cyrus was seventy years old when the mists of old age covered his face, and gray hair replaced his reddish hair.

One day when he was taking a rest, he dreamed of an angel, who warned him, "Prepare yourself, Cyrus. Soon you will be with God."

When this magnanimous man woke up, he knew the time of his emerging had come. In following his religious beliefs, he took an animal to the top of the mountains and sacrificed it. He prayed for his children, his friends, and the country that he loved. He returned to his palace and rested in the bed some more.

At the usual time, the housemaid informed him that the hot bath was ready. He responded that he would prefer to rest. At the designated time, the maid told him that supper was ready. He replied that it was not appetizing, but he asked for some water, which he enjoyed drinking. Day after a day, his condition remained the same. On the third day, he asked his children, his friends, the council members, and the heads of tribes to come to see him. There, as they gathered, Cyrus advised everyone to maintain the traditions with dignity, as well as the high moral standards.

He said, "My children, friends, and dignitaries, my final days are here upon me, and I can feel the symptoms. After my death, you must recognize me as a prosperous person. You can tell the story of my childhood, my youth, and my adulthood, that in each level, I was blessed and fortunate. My country before me was an unknown state in Asia; now, as I am dying, it is the largest country in the world. I do not remember losing any territory that I conquered. On the contrary, nations have volunteered to become part of my kingdom. My life passed exactly the way that I wanted it to pass, but I was always frightened of a defeat that would make God unhappy with me. I have never acted too proudly or arrogantly, nor did I act out of ordinary joy or happiness. Now that I am at my last days, I am happy to see you children alive and to leave my country and my friends prosperous. It would be rightful that every time you remember me, remember a person who achieved all that he wanted to accomplish.

"Today, I have to announce my successor so that after I am gone, there will be no division among you. My sons, I love you both the same, but I have to follow our tradition, leaving the kingdom to my oldest son. In our country, I have seen younger brothers prefer to follow their older brothers in walking, eating, talking, and seating from their childhood, which makes it easier to make my decision.

"My children, from childhood, I taught you to respect your elders, as your youths must respect you. Create a life in coordination with our laws, our customs, and our ethics. Therefore, Cambyses, you own the kingdom, and you, Bardiya—I give you Media, Caducean, and Armenia. With these grants, even though your brother is the king, you will prosper as well."

"Cambyses, do not forget that to protect the kingdom is not only to carry the title but to maintain honesty and faithful friends. Be aware that loyalty is earned only through your kindness. If your deeds are honest, according with our traditions, your influence and strength will excel power, but if you think to harm others, you will lose the trust of the people.

"My children and friends, when I am gone, invite the Persians and the allies around my tomb to congratulate me, that from now on, I am secure and comfortable in the hands of God. Goodbye, my children. Goodbye, my friends and present or absent people of my country."

After these words, Cyrus the Great shook everyone's hand and then wore his mask. Soon after, he died.

The most glorious ceremony was organized by his children and friends to honor the life of a unique person, who changed the course of history by advancing the recognition of individuals' rights, lasting in history until today.

His mummified body was carried in a golden coffin and placed next to his wife, Cassandane, in Pasargadae, famous as the tomb of Cyrus.

The construction of this tomb, under the supervision and following the tastes of Cyrus himself, lasted approximately twenty years. It began around 550 BC and was completed in 530 BC. Despite the passing of 2,500 years and so many natural and human disasters befalling the tomb of this great man, it still remains strong and in good condition. This is due to the overwhelming mathematical knowledge of the engineers and the physical abilities of the builders, as well as unknown factors that hold the biers. The building was constructed on a two-floor system, one movable and one fixed, which has lasted to this day.

Inside the tomb, Cyrus's personal items, such as golden clothing, a golden sword, a golden cane, and other memorable items, hang on the walls.

A friend of Alexander, who companied him to Iran in his memorials, wrote of the distracting actions and plunder of Alexander in the Pasargadae Treasure.

"The tomb was one of the center attractions in a wide area of vegetation and trees. It was Alexander, who turned this beautiful sight into desolation. In his first pillage, he took the body of Cyrus half out of the coffin in a most disrespectful manner, and then he stole all items of any value from the tomb." Unfortunately, after Alexander's visit and later the Arabic attack, there is now nothing left to represent the mummified body of Cyrus the Great, the leader, who brought about the liberty in our history.

There are different death versions of Cyrus introduced by some Greek historians. The most popular, next to real version mentioned above, is that Cyrus was in love with Tomyris, the queen of a small country in the northwest of Iran. While at war, a soldier of the queen struck Cyrus, and three days later, Cyrus died.

It is obvious that the purpose of creating such a story was to insult, disgrace, and damage a character that was pure, kind, godly, and eminent—a character worthy of being mentioned in the Bible, by Plato, in laws, and so much more.

Cyrus was old and possessed the largest military force at the time. He did not need to participate in a war at his old age, and he would not have done. If a war was needed, one or two of his generals could have concluded the dispute and brought the queen over in handcuffs. We can see throughout his life that Cyrus was a logical-minded king; hence, this story does not match with his character.

After all, Cyrus planned for years to share a tomb with his wife, Cassandane, and all of his last years' movements led toward that plan and nothing else. Knowing Cyrus and knowing his character, such accusations are meaningless and do not logically feel correct or real.

Cyrus the Great died by natural causes, of old age, and there is no other stories that prove otherwise.

History and Historians, Before and After Cyrus

Many dedicated Greek historians gathered crucial parts of ancient history. Right or wrong, these historians have provided imperative knowledge, and without their efforts, we would not have had access to these essentials historical information.

History has showed us that majority of writings have been tilted one way or another to please the writers' motives; the works of the Greek historians cannot be an exception. There are many contradicting versions. Some writers used fair assessments, while others tinkered with the events to impress or to express their national grace and pride. Descriptions of events or persons that are accurate seemingly often become twisted and in error, beyond the truth and the facts. Such one-sided history often created unreal views about the existence of a great civilization originated by the Persians and often portrayed them as barbaric or uncivilized throughout the ancient world and beyond.

This historical bias was planted by some Greek historians for various reasons, the most obvious being the preservation of their national pride. Therefore, some Greek historians wrote descriptions of events however they desired, without consideration for honestly. To make matters worse, there are no versions from Persian historians available to compare the facts, as witnessed by either side. If there ever were such versions, Alexander burned them, along with thousands of other books, in Persepolis when he became victorious. Such a one-sided history has created a fantasized environment full of exaggerated stories.

Some dishonest and shameful writers covered up the truth and claimed that the Persians were uncivilized and tyrannical or gave them other disadvantageous traits, creating a bias against the Persians throughout history. Discovery after discovery from various historical sites in Persepolis, Pasargadae, Ecbatana, and fields in Iran show the exact opposite perspective—that a level of sophistication and amazing math skills existed in the Persian Empire, countering the views of some envious Greek writers.

The misinterpreted meaning of the word *barbaric*, which the Greeks used to describe the Persians, created massive confusion throughout history, beside the vicious ideas of some writers. Today, *barbaric* means primitive, wild, uneducated, or even savage. The meaning of barbaric for the Greeks, however—, which they called the Persians during their two-century domination—originated from people speaking different languages. It had nothing to do with one's education, intellect, or behavior. Most Greek historians and philosophers knew the high level of intelligence in the Persian Empire, and they indicated the existence of such sophistication in their works.

The famous Greek philosopher Plato, and his The Laws is another example of existing sophistication, secular code of laws, freedom, freedom of speech and liberty throughout the Persians Empire. Unfortunately, some kind of misleading and bias has been preventing their contributions to be known as there is limited knowledge revealed about them.

Nevertheless, with regard to the ancient Iran and Greek affairs, here is a view from a brilliant military man in modern history, Napoleon.

"In the case of victories that Greeks are referring to facing a huge military of Xerox, we cannot forget that these words are coming from the Greeks. Boastful claims and exaggerations are clearly obvious."

This brief section was to clarify some trash talk and writings about the first civilization in human history, some fantasized versions of Greek storytelling, and the exaggerated one-sided stories told in motion pictures in our modern world.

To close this section, it's necessary to mention the names of a few Greek historians or writers of the time. Right or wrong, true or false, the honest or dishonesty of a writer lies in his work, as it would be for the following names:

- Hecataeus (550–476 BC). He lived part of his life during Cyrus the Great's lifetime. He was a Greek who was involved with the Persian satrap in Lydia.

- Herodotus (489–425 BC). He earned the title of the "father of history" by writing many books on various topics, especially about Cyrus. His accuracy has been controversial, as his aim was to give pleasure and provide exciting storytelling

- Xenophon (431–354 BC). He was a student of Socrates and a friend and classmate of Plato. His fascination with Cyrus the Great enabled him to write the *Cyropaedia*, a partly fictional biography of Cyrus, which became a favorite of Alexander, Julius Caesar, and many other leaders in history, including the modern world—Thomas Jefferson owned two copies. The *Cyropaedia* inspired the Founding Fathers in the United States to write the Constitution.

- Ctesias (late fifth century BC). He was the physician of Darius ll.
- Strabo (63 BC–AD 23). He lived during transition period between the Roman Republic and the Roman Empire.
- Plutarch (AD 46–120). He lived very close to end of ancient history during the Roman Empire.

Words of Wisdom by Cyrus the Great

Are you prepared to be free and happy, or do you want to always work hard without happiness?

My country before me was an unknown state in Asia. Now that I am dying, it is the largest country in the world.

My military has a policy that soldiers are free to express their opinions regarding the matters in a battle.

Honor women and respect them.

All humans are created equal; therefore, humankind is free to worship any god in whom a person is comfortable believing.

Let people of every tribe speak their native language freely.

My wish is to free the slaves and to esteem the wisdom of the wise.

Let my coffin be carried by the best doctors and physicians so people will see that there was nothing any physician could have done to stop my death.

A person who runs the people out of their homes would not have a good future and would have sleepless nights.

On the way to my tomb, give away my worthies and my gold, so people will see that my unlimited amount of wealth could not save my life.

A leader who is not with people will have a miserable time at his falling day.

I established peace in Babel and other cities. I freed people from the yoke that they engaged. I returned comfort to agitated and disturbed houses, ended tragedy in their lives, and ended their disastrous conditions.

A leader who does not know how the people's night ends to the sunrise is a grave digger, giving his heart to ignorance.

I promote liberty, freedom, and justice for all and defeat tyranny.

Place my hands out of my coffin for people to see that I did not take anything with myself to the other world.

CHAPTER 7

Buildings and Arts

Architecture and Engineering

Throughout Cyrus's realm and those of other Persian Empire kings, many wondrous constructions were built that still stand strong, after 2,500 years. Earthquakes, natural disasters, and the passage of time had no or little effect on them. These palaces, salons, gates, tombs, temples, and statues indicate there must have been super-intelligence among the Persian architects and engineers. They must have been highly skilled in mathematics, geometry, aerologic, and other scientific methods related to moving heavy blocks of stones and elevating them, as needed, without a crane, lifter, or other technological equipment of today.

Persepolis, Iran

Other amazing remains worth mentioning are the existence of so many inscriptions from the Persian kings. It appears that it was customary for the kings to leave inscriptions to identify them and to write a message of what they had done. These writings are scattered around various cities in today's Iran, as well as other cities in the Middle East. Some of those cities are Hamadan, Kermanshah, Shiraz, and Shush, to name a few.

Persepolis, Iran

Buildings were built with two layers on a floor. The first layer was unmovable and fixed, while the second layer was movable, to withstand the shocks of potential earthquakes. This method is used today to construct nuclear power plants.

Artistic Masterpieces Created during the Persian Empire

Numerous discovered masterpieces indicate an extraordinary lifestyle throughout the Persian Empire. Rare masterpieces are kept in various museums around the world.

Subjects for statues, articles, objects, or drawings include animals such as a lion, cow, boar, deer, rabbit, mountain goat, eagle, or other animal, as well as people. Articles made for personal use to follow religious beliefs or for decoration were extremely important to the Persian kings. A rare golden object was found in Shush—an image of the sun is visible, with two clouds behind it—and is now kept in the Louvre Museum in Paris today.

Around 1950, news of an important discovery amazed the ancient experts. This Middle Eastern discovery was in regard to some people accidentally finding a treasure full of golden objects that was transported to India. These golden pieces were important not only because of their historical value but because of their elegance, which gives them a unique value. Because of their style, scientists recognized this treasure as belonging to the Persian kings, meaning Cyrus, Darius, Xerxes, or others, said Farshad Abrishami, quoting from the London news.

This treasure is among the most expensive items in the British Museum today. Abrishami said that in 1923, two gold blocks found in Hamadan and two others found in 1933 in Persepolis, along with very fine rings, earrings, and necklaces, reflected the lifestyle of the time; there also was a statue of a camel and an eagle. He also said that at the end of the nineteenth century, the discovery process began by experts from England and France.

In 1849, Sir Kenneth Loftus of England, lasting until 1853, began the first official search. During this time, many monumental objects were found and transported to England. In 1885, Marcel Dieulafoy of France obtained a permit to excavate in Shush. He recovered many valuable and unusual articles, including twenty-one soldiers of the Persian Empire and impressions of lions and cows that were transported to the Louvre.

The discovery process in past two centuries recovered many golden masterpieces in various parts of Iran; these are mostly kept in the European museums, from the Louvre to Leningrad and others, reflecting the history of the mighty Persian Empire.

Abrishami also said that in 1895, another excavation permit

was granted to France for twelve years, but this excavation did not take place because of local protests and the unwillingness of Khuzestan's governor. However, in 1900, in Azerbaijan and Mazandaran, excavations continued, and many valuables were transported to the Louvre.

These wondrous, monumental pieces of gold, silver, and copper were found in Shush, Pasargadae, Persepolis, Kashan, Damghan, Azerbaijan, and Hamadan, as well as in other parts of Iran and Mesopotamia.

Remains of Pasargadae Palace, Iran

SOURCES

Abrishami, Farshad. Kourosh e Kabir-Tehran, Khaneh e Tarikh wa Taveer e Abrishami.

A. Dandamayev, Muhammad. Tarikh e Siyasi e Hakhamanishian-Translated by Bahari, Khashayar-Tehran, Karang.

Frye-Nelson, Richard. Miras e Baston e Iran-Translated by Rajabnia, Masoud-Tehran, Elmi wa Farhangi.

Gideons International. The Holy Bible-Nashville, TN: The Gideons International, 2013

Herodotus. The History of Herodotus-Translated by Rawlinson, George-London, J. M. Dent, 1910.

Lamb, Harold. Kourosh e Kabir-Translated by Shafeq, Rizazadeh, Sawdeq-Tehran, Sepehr Adab.

Khalyli, Abbas/Mahnaz. Kourosh e Bozorg-Tehran, Negah.

Myers, P.V.N. Ancient History, New York, Ginn & Company, 1916.

Nasri-Hamedani, Mosa. Eshq wa Saltanat-Tehran, Avaie Mahdees

Neya-Soltan, Ali/Shamsuldeeni Sajad. Kourosh e Kabir wa Dariuoush-Tehran, Arvand.

Panah-Muhammad, Behnam. Zendegginameh e Kourosh e Bozorg-Tehran, Sabzan.

Zarghamee, Riza. Discovering Cyrus-Washington, DC: Mage, 2013.

Printed in the United States
by Baker & Taylor Publisher Services